THE SPIDER:
THE SONG OF DEATH

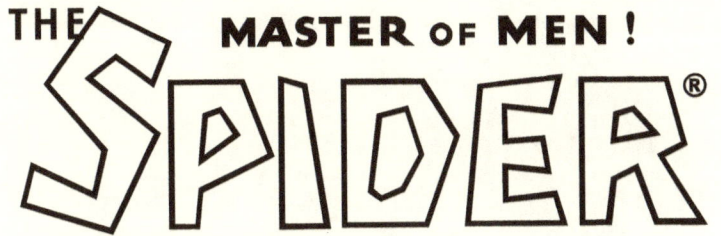

THE SONG OF DEATH

By Grant Stockbridge

POPULAR PUBLICATIONS · 2022

PUBLISHING HISTORY

"The Song of Death" originally appeared in the February 1939 (Vol. 17, No. 1) issue of
The Spider magazine. Copyright 2022 by Argosy Communications, Inc. All rights
reserved.

CHAPTER 1
THE BELLS OF HELL

RICHARD WENTWORTH shook his head dolefully. His strong, vitally handsome face was heavy with mock sorrow and his square, athlete's shoulders drooped in despondent resignation as he glanced at his wrist watch and sighed.

"If we're lucky, we should get there in time to catch a handful of rice—or maybe a stray slipper," he said—then glanced up with feigned, wide-eyed amazement as Nita van Sloan slipped into the evening wrap her maid held for her. Smiling, she came toward him.

"Remember, Dick," she protested, laughing, "we were not actually invited to open the church—but simply to witness the ceremony. I'm ready now—if you still want to escort me."

But the playful jesting was suddenly gone from Wentworth's face. It had been wiped away by that tingling something that gripped his heart and filled him with mingled awe and happiness whenever he beheld Nita like this. Her radiant loveliness took his breath away, brought a gleam of delighted admiration into the depths of his deep-set, blue-gray eyes. The look in his eyes, the touch of his fingers on her arm—as he led her out to the elevator—were more eloquent than any oral compliment.

They made a striking couple, those two. The elevator man smiled after them as they walked across the lobby of the River-

1

side Towers; the doorman smiled as he ushered them to Wentworth's waiting limousine—but the smile that Jackson, the chauffeur, turned upon them was one of pure adoration. To him, the "Major"—whom he had served in France—was the embodiment of male perfection, and Nita van Sloan, his fiancée, a goddess mate fit for such a man.

Noiselessly the powerful limousine moved away from the curb and started down Riverside Drive. Traffic was light for this hour of the evening. Jackson had the road to himself for half a dozen blocks, and into his mind came memories of other nights when he had driven these two—nights when death rode close behind them; when he had hunched over the wheel while Wentworth, in the grim role of the Spider, traded lead with enemies that closed in from every side....

Perhaps it was this momentary lapse into reminiscence that blinded Jackson to the swift approach of two automobiles. They were almost abreast of the limousine before he realized their presence. Two dark sedans that fairly leaped over the pavement. The instant he glimpsed them in the rear-view mirror an instinctive alarm clamored in his brain. Nerves tingling, his knuckles whitened on the wheel. He stepped on the gas—but already he was too late!

One of the cars had nosed abreast, spurted past, and veered to the right directly in his path. The other was alongside, was swinging in; driving him to the curb—over it—up onto the sidewalk!

In the same split-second the muzzle of a machine gun nosed from the rear window of the car ahead; another snouted from the sedan at his side. The gun ahead burst into flame, sewed a line of multi-spined stars across the shatter-proof glass windshield, hammered against the metal. Now the one in the side car would go into action— and that seam of lead would be stitched through Jackson's body....

He tensed, expecting the blast of searing agony that would be his end—then the sound of shots came from *behind* him. A sound he knew well—the sharp *crack-crack* of Wentworth's automatics!

Bullets whipped from the sedan alongside, but the chatter of the tommy gun, when it came, was a futile, short-

Over the church fell the death-dirge!

lived thing. Its staccato sputter ended in a shrill scream and the deadly muzzle dropped back into the car that was now scraping running-boards with the limousine.

Jackson jammed his foot on the brakes, but the heavy limousine catapulted across the sidewalk, straight for an iron railing that it would rip apart like tissue paper. Beyond that railing was the edge of a steep cliff—an almost sheer death-drop that could not be avoided once the car's wheels went over the edge.

An infinitesimal fraction of time separated them from eternity, but in that instant Jackson whipped the machine side-wise and plowed, head-on, into a concrete bench that was imbedded in the ground.

WENTWORTH HAD anticipated that desperate maneuver. Flinging himself in front of Nita, he braced and caught her body as the impact flung her forward. At the same moment the doors flew open—and then he was out on the edge of the cliff, crouching behind the settling, metallic-groaning wreckage. His twin automatics lanced flames at half a dozen dark figures who now rushed him from where the sedans had skidded to a tire-squealing stop.

"Flat on the floor!" he barked at Nita, then leaped up to the front of the machine, where Jackson dazedly struggled to open the jammed door.

A tommy gunner had the chauffeur squarely covered. But before he could press the trigger, Wentworth's bullet smashed through his forehead and hurled him back against the fellow running up behind him. That shot brought immediate repri-

4

sal. Bullets slapped against the limousine's heavy-plated sides, ricocheted crazily.

But the steady crackle of shots from Wentworth's gun were deadly.

One thug howled in agony as he was flung back into the gutter. Another cursed, dropping his gun and clutching his side. A third pitched forward on his face, lay still. The remaining two hesitated—and Wentworth's lead fairly lashed them back to their cars. Barely waiting for their wounded companions to climb in, they slammed the doors. Then the sedans dashed off into the night.

Police whistles were now shrilling.

The gun battle had taken no more than a few, scant minutes, but in that time at least two men had died, and others had left a trail of blood to attest the unerring accuracy of Richard Wentworth's arms.

He stepped to the rear door of the limousine, his taut face anxious. But Nita was already stepping out.

"I'm all right, Dick," she reassured him. "Was Jackson hurt?"

"A fine bump on the head," Jackson answered bitterly, coming around the machine, a handkerchief pressed against his bleeding forehead. "That's all—just a bump. It ought to be worse—me driving so easy into that trap!"

A bluecoat came running toward them, revolver in hand; and awe-stricken spectators, who had stood frozen with terror, now timidly yielded to curiosity, edged forward. Wentworth stepped across the path to the first of the prone figures. The man was dead—Cully Katz, a mobster well known as a henchman of Heinie Schneider's.

Wentworth's eyes narrowed, his lips clamping tight. He stepped to the tommy-gunner whom he had bull's-eyed through the forehead—and the hard, straight line of his mouth became even more grim. This fellow was Tony Lorenzo—and still another of the Schneider mobsters.

The identity of those Schneider killers was the explanation for this death-trap....

FOR MORE than six months District Attorney Kenneth Baker had been conducting an anti-racket crusade whose climax had come with the prosecution of Heinie Schneider, three of his lieutenants and one James Leary, a powerful political leader. Schneider and his mates had been charged with waging a murderous racketeer campaign against the city's personal loan corporations.

Leary had been accused of being his protector and cover.

The trial, finished this very afternoon, had resulted in the conviction of Schneider and two of his lieutenants—but also of the acquittal of Leary and "Angel" McCabe, the fifth defendant. Richard Wentworth had been highly instrumental in securing those convictions. Fighting the mobsters with their own weapons, he had donned the ebon habiliments of the Spider and, meeting them in their own lairs, had finally succeeded in driving them out into the open.

Several of those contacts had not been made in his Spider disguise, and it also had been necessary for him to appear personally as a damaging witness against the racketeers at the trial. At the time, Schneider had darkly hinted at vengeance… and now this vicious attack, Wentworth realized, was the gang boss' swift reprisal.

"There are two of your men, officer," Wentworth indicated the corpses to the policeman. "The rest got away in their machines. Their cars were more fortunate than mine." He regarded the wrecked limousine ruefully. "They smashed us up beautifully—tried to drive us over the cliff, as you can see."

The officer was impressed by this capable-looking, authoritative man in perfectly fitting evening clothes. However, a gun battle and two corpses in the middle of Riverside Drive were matters for which he could not personally assume responsibility. "You'll have to stay here, sir," he stated flatly, although Wentworth had made no attempt to leave. "I'll have to call the captain. You can't leave till he comes. I'm gonna stay here," he decided. "You—" to a gaping-mouthed onlooker, "run down to the call-box, corner after next, and notify the station about this. Step on it."

There was nothing to do but wait. Nearly ten minutes elapsed before a police car sirened up to the curb and the precinct captain got out. He recognized Wentworth at once.

"You had a mighty narrow escape, sir," he muttered as he looked down at the dead killers and then turned faintly admiring eyes on Wentworth's tall, lithe-muscled figure. "Looks as if those rats won't lose any time squaring things for Heinie. Certainly, you can go now, Mr. Wentworth. There are no charges against you. It doesn't look as if we'll even need your testimony—unless we locate the rest of this gang."

That, Wentworth decided privately, was a very slim possibility. But he left Jackson with the wrecked limousine to give any other information the police might want. Nita and he took a taxi to the church; and as they got out in front of fashionable St. Stephen's, they heard the deep rumble of the organ pealing out the wedding march.

The Robinson-Eaton nuptials were already in progress. The procession was moving down the aisle and the ushers at the doors barred any further guests. Nita and Wentworth had to be content with places in the vestibule from which they could watch the bride going to meet her groom.

TINY AND fragile-looking beside her tall, gray-haired father, Grace Robinson advanced to where Assistant District Attorney Charles Eaton and his best man stood beside the minister. This was a proud day in Eaton's life, Wentworth knew. Young ADA Eaton had had a leading part in the successful prosecution of the Schneider case, and now he was about to wed the beautiful daughter of Joab Robinson, one of New York's leading social and financial figures.

A proud and happy day... Eaton stood smiling in front of the altar, at the end of the aisle that divided a sea of smiling, approving faces. A lovely wedding... Stirringly the notes of the organ swelled out the familiar melody—and then suddenly Wentworth's brows wrinkled and he cocked his head to one side, listening frowningly.

No, he had not been mistaken. Through the resounding

tones of Mendelssohn, rising thinly above the familiar melody, he caught a weird, wailing, minor theme. It became stronger, more undeniable, as he listened. Now it was competing with the march, was beginning to drown it out.

There was something strangely, hauntingly familiar about that weird dirge. Now Wentworth recognized it, and was startled by its peculiar significance....

Less than a year ago, Grace Robinson had been engaged to a young aviator named Russell Gillespie. Their engagement had been terminated abruptly, and soon after that she had been betrothed to Charles Eaton. The breaking-off had created a seven day social flurry and had then been forgotten—by everyone except young Gillespie. He had taken his dismissal very much to heart and, soon after, had set out on a solo trans-Atlantic flight.

His plane had been lost at sea, nothing but an oil spot on the waves remaining to tell of his fate—and then it was discovered that his had been a suicide flight. Behind him he had left a farewell note to Grace, written on the back of a sheet of music copy paper on which he had composed a weird melody. "The Song of Death" the newspapers had dubbed it.

And that was the melody now pealing through the church! Russell Gillespie's death-song at Grace Robinson's wedding!

The audience, Wentworth saw, had now recognized it, also. The smiles were fading from their faces. Tense and frightened looking, they glanced at one another then back to the slow-marching procession. The principals, too, realized its significance. Color blanched from their cheeks as the eerie tune grew in volume. Something, they sensed, was terribly wrong. But they little suspected the rapidly approaching climax of that uncanny melody.

Now it was booming forth in notes that filled the whole church, that beat into their ears; was mounting in a jarring, crashing crescendo that widened their eyes with agonized horror as it rocked their brains. Consternation, agony... and then utter madness flashed in kaleidoscopic succession over their faces!

In an instant the staid, ultra-fashionable church became a madhouse—a madhouse in which all the inmates were loose, clawing and tearing at one another horribly in frantic struggle to escape! Fascinated, rooted by horror to the spot on which he stood, Wentworth stared at that savage mêlée, that hellish battle-royal. Men and women shredding one another's clothing from their bodies, clawing the flesh from their faces—screaming and howling in a bedlam that drowned the echoes of that last terrible note!

That maniacal struggle seemed to go on forever, yet a few seconds after it started, the wild-eyed, mask-faced combatants were falling all over the church—going down with that utter limpness that betokened death even before their bodies hit the floor!

Only then did Wentworth realize that his senses were reeling; only now was he conscious of the terrible pain that seemed to be cramming his brain with agony until its very volume threatened to split his skull wide open. He glanced at Nita and saw the agony in her contorted face, the awful, nameless terror in her violet eyes. She stood there, powerless to defend herself against this mad melody....

By a supreme effort of will that drenched his body with perspiration, Wentworth wrenched himself from that death trance, forced his paralyzed muscles to life.

"Nita!" He grabbed her waist, half-carried, half-dragged her from the vestibule and out into the street.

Here the blessed quiet closed in around them, as if bathing them from head to foot in some humane, soothing medicament. Wentworth felt the madness ebbing from him, felt the ringing in his head subsiding, the tingling in his veins fading.

Propped against the side of the building, Nita held her head, moaning softly.

"Oh, God—Dick! What happened?" Her voice came in a hoarse whisper. "What *was* it?"

But Wentworth had no answer for that question. Still shaken, he watched a score of survivors stagger from the church doors and fall, writhing, to the pavement. A score of survivors of all the hundreds who were gathered in that temple of God! It was incredible, unthinkable, too appalling to be possible—yet it was true!

Except for the few who had been close to the doors or in the vestibule, there had been no escape whatsoever. The bride and groom, bridesmaid and best man, clergyman and all the members of the wedding party lay where they had fallen, horribly intermingled with the contorted forms of nearly five hundred guests!

Richard Wentworth stood in the doorway of that newly made

charnel house and gazed with incredulous, horrified eyes at the most ghastly sight he had ever seen. A few short minutes ago this church had been a shrieking riot; now the pall of the grave hung over it....

CHAPTER 2
DEATH CALLS TWICE

THE WAIL of police sirens echoed through that great sepulcher like eldritch banshee screams and they served to jerk Wentworth back to some semblance of normalcy. Radio cars were swarming in from every direction. Blue-coated figures leaped from them, came running toward the church doors. There had been an officer on guard outside the building, Wentworth remembered; no doubt he had sent in a frantic alarm the moment he realized this inexplicable tragedy was far past the handling of one lone guardian of the law.

Help had come.

Now a police cordon was thrown around the church to hold back the gathering crowd and to prevent anyone from leaving until the "accident" had been thoroughly investigated. The first captain to arrive on the scene strode into the building. For a moment he hesitated, nonplussed, then walked down the aisle and grabbed one of the sprawled figures by the shoulder. He shook it curiously, impatiently. The man's head rolled to one side. His mouth sagged open; glazed eyes stared up sightlessly from a horror-mask of a face—and the captain sprang back as if his hand had been dipped into virulent acid.

"God, he's dead!" he gasped, white-faced, as the enormity of what he had discovered dawned upon him. "They're *all* dead! This is a case for the commissioner!" He hurried off to notify headquarters.

Silence....

Ashen-faced, the officers clustered in the doorways and stared in at that ghastly scene, remaining at the threshold as if merely to step into the church would be to cross into the perilous unknown of the grave world. Then suddenly the astounded watchers tensed with clammy terror, grasping instinctively for their guns as cold chills now ran up and down their spines.

There was *one* living man in that corpse host! There, coming up the center aisle, was a figure that picked its way carefully between the piled-up bodies! A tall, thin, Vandyked figure in evening clothes; a studious, professorial figure who seemed quite unmoved by this holocaust around him!

"I am Fleming Trask, the organist," he answered their startled questions, as he reached the doorway. "I was on my bench, playing the wedding march, when this happened."

"And you came out of there alive?" a police sergeant muttered incredulously. "You were up there in the middle of it—but you lived through it? How did *you* escape?"

"I know nothing about it, gentlemen." The organist shook his head. "I was concentrating on my music. I knew nothing until my organ mirror revealed the horror that was suddenly transpiring behind me."

Wentworth had been quick to notice the curious way the man's eyes were glued to his questioner's lips.

13

"You heard nothing?" Wentworth interjected swiftly. "You did not hear that weird melody that drowned out the wedding march?"

"I heard nothing whatever, gentlemen." Trask shook his head, and a half-smile touched his thin features. "You see—*I am stone deaf.*"

Stone deaf! That, of course, would explain his miraculous escape—if the deaths actually had been tied up with *hearing* that penetrating melody. But it might also explain why the organist could have played the role of murderer with complete safety. That "Song of Death" must have come from the organ. From where else could it have come? But the whole idea was so bizarre, so fantastic, it bordered on the preposterous—a musician murdering a church full of people simply by playing a death song!

The police were still questioning Trask when Police Commissioner Stanley Kirkpatrick arrived accompanied by District Attorney Kenneth Baker. A handsome, florid-faced man in his late forties, Kirkpatrick was, as always, immaculate in his evening clothes, a small gardenia adorning the lapel of his dinner jacket. Years of command had given him an air of authority, a complete confidence, that could not be easily shaken. Yet the color drained from his cheeks as he beheld the horror awaiting him....

His startlement was nothing compared to that of the bull-dog-faced little district attorney. Baker's eyes widened like saucers, and tiny beads of perspiration oozed agonizingly out on his forehead.

"Dead—every one of them dead!" he repeated, as if trying to convince himself of something all logic rejected. "And I ought to be lying there among them, Kirk! I escaped death by a miracle. If it had not been for the Luderman case—I cursed my luck because I had to stay in the office to question him and so miss Charlie's wedding—but that's all that saved my life. Otherwise, I should be here with the other guests!"

"Probably it is really why they were killed—because you were expected to be here with them." Kirkpatrick's narrowed eyes flashed around the corpse-littered church—and fell upon Richard Wentworth.

"Dick!" His expression tightened.

"Nita and I were supposed to be in there, also," Wentworth said quietly. "We owe our lives to another miracle—one that I believe Heinie Schneider had something to do with." Quickly he recounted the murderous automobile attack that had proved to be their salvation.

Kirkpatrick's saturnine features grew bleak as he listened, his eyes cold as steel.

"Damn them!" he swore softly. "Schneider—or more likely Jim Leary. That's where the responsibility lies! Leary is behind every move that Schneider makes, no matter what any blind jury might decide. That jury was dismissed at three-fifteen this afternoon—yet already two of the state's chief witnesses have been murdered. Gus Meyers was fool enough to step up to a bar in his own neighborhood an hour after he left the courtroom. He went down with three bullets in him. Leo Umhoefer was run down two hours later. He tried to get out of the way of a truck, then a taxi smashed him against an elevated pillar. He was almost *decapitated.*"

He raged. "Brazen, deliberate murder flung right into our faces! We know it—but try to prove it to a soft-headed jury! Now *this...*" he came back to the horror before him. "Five hundred people murdered, in order to punish Baker and Eaton for their prosecution! Schneider's mob has gone murder-mad. But this time they have overstepped themselves. An outrage like this cannot be perpetrated without leaving clues. We'll nail them sure!"

That was what Stanley Kirkpatrick wanted to believe—but very soon it became apparent that he had been overly optimistic. The

There was a terrific explosion that shook the ground with such force that Wentworth was knocked flat!

16

police searched the church building from top to bottom, yet not a single clue could they uncover. Not a trace of the way the mass-murder had been accomplished or of the identity of its perpetrator....

WHILE NITA waited in an anteroom, Wentworth joined in that grisly search. Sick with horror, he watched the bodies of the victims being removed by the ambulances and quickly requisitioned trucks that had arrived by the dozens. Carefully he fine-combed the choir loft and the organist's station—but not one clue could he find.

Fleming Trask was the only possible lead on which the police could work, but he promised to be of small help. He had told his story, which amounted to little more than nothing; nor did he add or detract anything upon cross-examination. He had played the Mendelssohn wedding march; he had seen nothing at all until the wedding guests began dropping dead all over the church like flies. The police finally took him downtown for further questioning, but that, Wentworth felt, was but a forlorn hope.

"I can't hold him," Kirkpatrick admitted. "You can't hold a man on suspicion of murder merely because he happened to be playing an organ when a lot of people dropped dead. We'd be laughed out of court. Besides, I don't believe that he had a thing to do with it. Leary and Schneider don't use people like Trask for *their* deviltry."

Wentworth was inclined to agree with that, yet he could not get the odd picture of Fleming Trask out of his mind.

"He looked like an apparition, like some gaunt keeper of

the dead, as he picked his way up the aisle," he mused to Nita, as a taxicab sped them to the Riverside Towers. "A deaf organist at the keyboard when the Song of Death drowns out the wedding music and turns the place into a morgue—the whole thing would be utterly fantastic if it weren't so ghastly!"

His thoughts were still back there in the church, when Nita unlocked the door of her apartment... but instantly he snapped out of his abstraction. Suddenly alert, some sixth sense flashed an electric warning to his brain. Danger was in his nostrils, was whispering in his ears, was tingling his every nerve. *Danger lay there in the darkness!*

Nita was inside, had her hand on the light switch before he could stop her. Her finger pressed the button, flooded the reception hall with light—but now he was in front of her in a cat-like bound that swept her back against the wall. He leaped past, flung himself, crouching low, through the living-room archway. That arrowlike dive was a marvel of muscular synchronization. All in one lightning-swift motion, he slapped his left hand up against the light switch—and pressed the trigger of the automatic in his right.

As the room flashed alight, he saw his mark—saw three of them. Seated in one of Nita's armchairs was a burly, fat-faced gorilla, an automatic in his pudgy fist held steady on the doorway. At the left, near an open window, was another thug. A third, a sleek-haired, rat-faced killer, leaned with studied negligence against the bedroom of Nita's doorway.

Wentworth's shot was echoed by the three others that blended with it. Two of their bullets lanced harmlessly through the archway. The other, from the gun of the man in the chair, went wild and shattered a picture on the wall above Wentworth's head— for now it was the finger of a dead man that pulled the trigger.

Instantly Wentworth's aim shifted. But the shower of glass that deluged him had thrown him momentarily off-balance. His second shot caught the fellow at the window, brought a gasp of pain from him, as his gun dropped to the floor. The fellow had been swift to realize his danger. Even as the bullet plowed into his shoulder, his foot came up beneath a small table and sent it and the books it held sailing across the room.

Wentworth ducked the table, warded off the books with his outthrust arm—but one of the book-ends caught him on the side of the head and spun him half-way around. Now there were two guns in his hands—two guns that were blazing twin death....

But his targets had flown. Warned by the swift fate of their companion, they had waited for no more. The wounded man leaped to the fire-escape behind him, scampered out of sight. The other had dived into the bedroom.

Warily Wentworth crept to the window and made certain that the wounded man was not lurking outside on the landing. Then, assured that Nita was safe from a rear-attack, he edged his way cautiously to the bedroom door and darted through it. But the killer had gone. He had slipped into the bathroom and out through a narrow window from which he could catch hold of the fire-escape ladder.

Two of them had escaped—but the man in the chair slumped, head on chest. Curiously Wentworth lifted the head, tilted it to one side. This time recognition gave him no surprise. As he had expected, the dead man was another of Schneider's gangsters—Hoppy Lewis, a bruiser belonging to the kingpin's bodyguard.

Now there was no mistaking the source of these attacks or the persistent and very real danger they presented.

"You can't stay here, Nita," Wentworth decided quickly. "This makes three escapes in one night. Our luck can't hold out forever. It seems they are after you as well as me. I don't want you to be alone for a minute. Pack some things in a bag, and I'll take you back to Sutton Place with me as soon as the police arrive."

While she packed, he telephoned Stanley Kirkpatrick at police headquarters. Ten minutes later the police were there to take his statement and remove Lewis' body. Now he and Nita were free to leave the apartment that had so nearly proved their death trap.

Wentworth could not understand why the trap had been set for them. On the way to Sutton Place, he tried to figure it out; tried to reconcile the puzzling events of the evening. This latest trap might have been quickly staged because he and Nita had escaped the fate that had awaited them in St. Stephen's church. But why had they been waylaid by those gangster-filled sedans on their way to the wedding? Why had they not been allowed to go straight to the church, arrive on scheduled time and be killed with the others?

The thing didn't make sense; seemed to be at cross-purposes. The more he thought about it, the more he became convinced that he must have another look at that church and its organ without delay.

Once Wentworth had Nita safely within the protection of his own headquarters he breathed more easily. Built partly on two piers that projected into the East River, partly on the shore behind them, the place was a veritable fortress—a stronghold that could be approached through its own grounds or by way of an apartment in one of the buildings in front of it on Sutton Place. Equipped with steel doors and shutters, guarded by every modern defense device, it had been made as nearly attack-proof as human ingenuity could manage.

There Nita would have the protection of dependable Jackson; of tall, bearded Ram Singh, the Sikh personal man who served Wentworth with utter devotion; of old Jenkyns, the valet who had served Wentworth's father before him—a trio of faithful attendants who were far more than servants. They were tried and true friends, each one of them; friends and comrades who were ready to lay down their lives for Richard Wentworth and for the woman he loved.

"Look after her until I return," he told them—and then he was off on a return trip to that blood-drenched church that was already an object of citywide horror.

THE BIG Gothic building was dark when he approached it. The doors were closed, and a police guard had been posted. To try to gain entrance that way would be useless. However, the church stood on a corner. It could be entered from the side street—and now there seemed to be no policemen on duty there.

Wentworth went down that street and returned on the church

side, approaching it from the rear. Striving to make himself as inconspicuous as possible, he was alert, tense, his eyes searching the shadows for the slightest betraying movement. Just ahead of him was the alleyway that ran behind the building. If he could reach that without being seen....

But suddenly a familiar-looking figure stepped out of the dark opening and glanced warily up and down the block.

That figure... Wentworth was on him in a flash, had him pinned back against the stone wall with an automatic jabbed into his ribs before he had a chance to make a sound. A tall, thin man with a Vandyke beard. Wentworth nodded with satisfaction.

"Thought you looked familiar, Trask," he said softly and slowly, so that the man could not miss the movement of his lips. "Perhaps the police will be interested to know that you came back to prowl around here, the moment they released you. But maybe you prefer to tell me what you were doing inside there. Which is it going to be? Speak up, man."

For a moment it seemed that Fleming Trask could not speak. He trembled from head to foot. His breath came in little gasps, and his face was a sickly white in the weak gleam of a nearby arc light.

"You don't understand... you don't understand!" he chattered frantically. "There are more dead men in there—policemen. Murdered policemen! Here, let me show you—right behind the building. You can see for yourself."

Wentworth allowed him to wriggle away from the barrel of the automatic, let him lead the way into the dark mouth of the alley to where something even darker lay heaped on the pavement. Taking a pencil-flash from his pocket, Wentworth turned its concentrated beam on that black heap—and it became the awkwardly huddled body of a policeman. A policeman with a broken head that had drenched his uniform with blood.

"There are more," the organist quavered. "I just came—"

And then his voice was lost in a terrific explosion that shook the ground with such violence that Wentworth was knocked flat. Instinctively he scrambled to his feet and fairly flung himself out into the street, just as part of the rear wall of the church came tumbling down in ruins. Stunned by the concussion, he poised there on his hands and knees and looked back. The entire rear end of the church had been demolished. It had fallen in on itself, completely burying the organ and everything near it.

The organ… That was why he had come there, to investigate the organ. But now it was impossible. Somebody had foreseen the probability of such an investigation and had thwarted it. Somebody….

Suddenly his dazed mind cleared and he remembered. Fleming Trask, the organist—where was he? Trask was gone, and when Wentworth turned the beam of his pocket-flash into the alleyway, he could see no sign of the man there.

The dust of the fallen masonry was still thick in the air, and already the alarm was being sounded. Police whistles were shrilling. Wentworth saw two patrolmen come running from the front of the building—and at that moment he spied a lanky figure that suddenly appeared from nowhere and sped down the block. Fleming Trask!

Wentworth was after him instantly. But those patrolmen coming from the avenue did not understand. They were yelling at him, calling to him to stop; and then he heard the bark of their revolvers. They were trying to stop him with bullets!

There was no time to stop, no time for explanations. He must keep after that long-legged fugitive now so desperately racing for the far corner. Wentworth was gaining, was within fifty feet of his quarry when the fleeing man reached the corner—and dived straight into the door of a coupé that opened to receive him!

The moment Trask was inside, the car leaped away from the curb. Warning shots whistled past Wentworth's ears to discourage pursuit, but he ignored them. Ducking low, he raced after the car, leaped onto the running-board. For just a moment he clung there—long enough to glimpse a terrified girl crouching over the wheel, a grim-faced man beside her holding Trask. Then the man leaned forward and lashed out of the window with a pistol barrel. It slapped against Wentworth's fingers, broke his hold—tumbled him off into the street.

Before he could scramble to his feet, the car was gone. With a wild careen, it swung around a corner, disappeared—and then he had to take to his heels to avoid the oncoming policemen....

CHAPTER 3
MELODY OF DOOM

POLICE COMMISSIONER Stanley Kirkpatrick sat at his desk the next morning and gloomily studied the enigmatic face he knew so well. Many a time before this he had tried to read behind those bland features—and his success so far, he privately admitted, was just about zero. Always perfectly poised and at his ease, when Richard Wentworth wanted to conceal his thoughts there was no clairvoyant who could hope to penetrate his poker mask.

Between these two there existed a friendship that was genuine, lasting—a friendship built on a basis of mutual respect, even though their codes differed.

By his whole life and training, Kirkpatrick was irrevocably committed to law and order. To him, the law was paramount; almost a deity. At times, he would admit, it might blunder, might be hamstrung, might seem to fail—but eventually it would triumph, without the aid of private agencies. Never, under his code, was a man justified in taking the law into his own hands. That was where he and Wentworth differed. That was where he and the Spider were uncompromisingly at loggerheads—and the Spider, he at times had shrewdly suspected, was no other than Richard Wentworth.

Stanley Kirkpatrick had never been able to prove that suspicion. Otherwise, Wentworth at that moment would have been in jail, facing the electric chair, instead of sitting in the commissioner's office. For Kirkpatrick there would be no compromise, no equivocating. He would have followed the path of duty even though it meant dooming his best friend.

"I know that you had nothing to do with that ghastly slaughter at St. Stephen's, Dick," the commissioner said thoughtfully, as he brushed his spiked mustache nervously with the first knuckle of his right hand. "However, I do think that you know a lot more about this outrage than you have admitted. You returned there last night. Two patrolmen saw and identified you. Perhaps I can reconstruct what happened. You went back there to see what you could discover. You got into the building, uncovered some lead—and then blew up the church to keep us from learning of your discovery." He eyed Wentworth shrewdly. "That was because you want to play a lone hand—"

"And for that reason I killed one of your men, Kirk?" Wentworth interrupted to ask.

For a long moment the commissioner was silent.

"Two patrolmen died there last night," he said then. "You did not kill them—and that is the only reason why I have not clapped you into jail on the testimony of the men who saw you running away from the church. But that does not mean that I cannot change my mind at any moment," Kirkpatrick glowered. "This is police business, Dick—remember that. I want no interference from the Spider. I will not *tolerate* any. Is that clear?"

"So clear that even the Spider should be able to understand it," Wentworth grinned.

Kirkpatrick seemed to accept that as a tacit promise, and the stern lines in his face relaxed.

"The physicians who autopsied the bodies of the church victims have been unable to discover any cause of death," he went on. "The cases baffle them, so I have turned to the psychologists for aid. Spencer Palmer, head of the New York Psychiatric Association, has undertaken an investigation and promised me a report at eleven this morning. Wait a bit and hear him."

The Spider was one thing to Stanley Kirkpatrick; but the help of Richard Wentworth, amateur dilettante criminologist, was another. On many occasions he and Wentworth had worked together, and now he was open to suggestions.

They had not long to wait. Dr. Spencer Palmer was announced in less than five minutes. He was square-shouldered, well-setup, about fifty, with a keen, intelligent face—a face that was characterized chiefly by a broad, high forehead and long upper lip. A man of emphatic opinions and sharp decisions, Wentworth estimated him. Yet now he seemed hesitant, almost apologetic.

"I have gone into this extraordinary case very thoroughly with several of my associates, Commissioner," he responded to Kirkpatrick's greeting. "Of course, we cannot be certain just what may have transpired there in the church last night. However, from all indications, I am inclined to the belief that the deaths may have been caused by mass hysteria. This may sound far-fetched to a layman, but there are on record many well-authenticated cases where considerable numbers of people have suddenly been gripped and stricken by crowd suggestion."

"Ignorant savages, perhaps," Kirkpatrick protested. "But, Doctor, these victims were men and women of superior intelligence and education. Do you tell me that five hundred people of that sort would become hysterical and drop dead?"

"I admit that there is no authenticated case of mass hysteria involving quite this number of deaths or among people of so high a caliber," Palmer admitted. "But there is no reason why, under the emotional stress that always attends a wedding, people of superior intelligence should not react similarly to their lesser brothers. There have been cases of wholesale prostrations in colleges that could be attributed to no other cause than this. There also have been cases—unauthenticated, I admit, but nonetheless possible—where whole towns in Europe have been inexplicably wiped out by mass prostration."

He went on. "Undoubtedly this is the most phenomenal case of its kind modern psychiatry has encountered. I am greatly interested in it, and I want to offer you every aid within my power."

Kirkpatrick thanked him, but the moment he had gone the commissioner admitted that he took no stock in such a wild theory.

"Mass hysteria!" he snorted. "That murderous outrage was planned and staged by nobody but Jim Leary in order to strike down Charles Eaton and the district attorney. But," he amended bitterly, "proving that is another matter. We have to go very slowly even in attempting to pin anything like that on Leary—"

The telephone interrupted, and Kirkpatrick reached for it.

"Yes—yes, Leland Chaney. Hello, Chaney," he spoke into the receiver, and Wentworth, sitting beside the desk, clearly heard a strident, rasping voice come over the wire.

Leland Chaney was the president of the many-branched New York Personal Loan Company. It was he who had led the revolt against the racketeers when they thrust their tentacles into the loan companies; he who made the complaint and furnished the evidence that started District Attorney Baker's drive. Throughout the trial he had been a courageous and invaluable witness for the State—but now he seemed to be in abject terror.

RICHARD WENTWORTH .

"You've posted a police guard outside my house, but what good are they?" Wentworth heard him demand. "I have been threatened over the telephone—twice last night and again this morning. They laugh at the police. They tell me I'm going to pay no matter how many cops are guarding me—and just now I received another threat. A crazy sheet of music paper with skulls instead of notes! They're going to kill me, Kirkpatrick—I know it!" his voice rose to a frightened, piercing squeal. "You and the district attorney promised to protect me, and you're letting me down! They'll get me just the way they got Meyers and Umhoefer—"

"Take it easy, Chaney," the commissioner's cool, hard voice knifed through the man's mounting hysteria. "We'll take care of you—don't worry about that. I'll have your police guard doubled immediately, and I am coming right up there to have a look at that music paper. Stay where you are. Don't move out of the house until I see you."

The telephone dropped back into its cradle, and Kirkpatrick turned to stare at Wentworth with a wordless question in his eyes.

"More of this death song," Wentworth clipped, "and the sooner we get up there the better."

Kirkpatrick grabbed the phone and ordered his car. Then he got the precinct in which Chaney lived and detailed half a dozen more men to guard the house. That was all he could do—but Wentworth had a peculiar presentiment that it was not going to be sufficient....

KIRKPATRICK WAS silent as his car sped uptown, but he sighed with relief when they turned off Fifth Avenue into East

31

Seventieth Street. There seemed to be no unusual excitement in front of Chaney's four-story mansion. They were in time!

Chaney was locked in his study, the scared-faced butler told them, as he led the way to a room at the rear of the second floor. Two more servants were on guard there, nervously clutching revolvers in hands that were obviously unfamiliar with the feel of firearms. They gladly gave way at sight of the blue uniforms behind the commissioner.

Kirkpatrick knocked on the door.

"All right, Chaney—open up. This is Kirkpatrick!" he called. But there was no answer—until Wentworth sprang to the door and put his ear against the panel.

From inside the study he caught the muffled strains of a melody he knew all too well—the Song of Death! And then Leland Chaney's voice, shrieking in terror, rising now into a wild, mad scream!

Wentworth flung himself at that door with all his strength, but it was built of solid wood. Not until two policemen joined him in a concerted rush were they able to snap it from its hinges... and then the weird music had ceased. Its work was done. Leland Chaney lay sprawled over his desk, his dead face contorted with mad agony. In his right hand he clutched a sheet of music copy paper....

Kirkpatrick drew it from the grasp of the relaxing fingers and flattened it on the desktop. A sheet of music paper with a devilish tune that almost seemed to cackle up at them from the hideous skulls that leered on the bars in place of notes. The *Song of Death*, Wentworth read the grisly scoring at a glance....

"Whatever killed him is here in this room!" the commissioner snapped. "Find it!"

Half a dozen detectives joined the search. They took down pictures, tore down wall panels, and ripped away every bit of woodwork that looked as if it might conceal even as much as a wire. They examined the furniture, took up the rug and went over every inch of the hardwood floor—but nowhere could they find a trace of hidden mechanism by which the song could have been introduced into the room.

Utterly baffled, Wentworth turned to where the commissioner paced the littered room.

"This is more mass hysteria, I suppose!" Kirkpatrick snorted. "I have had my car sent for Spencer Palmer. I want to hear what explanation he has to offer for this."

In a few minutes he had his answer. The psychiatrist walked into the room and stared down at the banker's body, scrutinized the twisted features carefully as he listened to what had occurred. Then he turned his attention to the skull note music score—frowned down at it.

"This does not coincide very well with my former theory, I admit," he conceded. "You are definitely certain that you heard this death song—even though you can find no wires or mechanism by which it could have been introduced into the room? Then I can only attribute this man's death to terror. He knew of the orgy of death last night in St. Stephen's. He had received threats, received this sheet of music that was preying on his mind. He may well have been so conditioned by terror that the sound of the melody served to kill him."

But how had the sound of that melody reached him?

That question was still unanswered when Kirkpatrick gave up the search, and Wentworth returned to Sutton Place. All during lunch Wentworth's restless brain labored with that problem. A radio broadcast seemed the most logical answer to it—and yet there had been no receiving mechanism… And what sort of demoniacal orchestration could produce that maddening pain he had felt stealing into his brain in St. Stephen's?

HE WAS still mulling over those questions that afternoon when Jenkyns announced a Miss Gillespie who wanted to speak with him on the phone. Miss Gillespie… Wentworth endeavored to place the name as he picked up the receiver. There was something familiar about it, and yet….

"Mr. Wentworth!" an anxious voice throbbed into his ear the moment he spoke into the instrument. "I am Joan Gillespie, the sister of Russell Gillespie—the aviator who was lost at sea."

Russell Gillespie!

Wentworth tingled with sudden excitement, and the girl seemed to divine his thoughts.

"Yes," she half-sobbed, "the composer of that awful Song of Death that is in all the newspapers. That is why I am calling you, Mr. Wentworth. I am in such terrible trouble; I don't know where to turn!"

"The police—" Wentworth started to say, but she cut him short.

"Oh, I *can't* go to the police!" Her voice rose in a despairing wail. "They would never listen to me. That's why I need your help and advice so badly. Oh, *please* don't turn me down!"

34

Russell Gillespie, the dead man whose memory had haunted the Robinson-Eaton wedding and plunged it into appalling tragedy...
And now his sister was calling for aid....

"You *will* see me!" the girl leaped at Wentworth's silence and construed it as consent. "You really *will* come to meet me?"

"Why can't you come here?" Wentworth countered.

"I don't dare!" her voice was again tinged with panicky anxiety. "I can't possibly get away long enough for that. I am in Woodside—only a short distance over the Queensborough Bridge. If you will come here I can slip out long enough to meet you in the Colonial Tavern. That's on the Boulevard and Forty-Eighth Street. I will be waiting in the back room—in the first booth beyond the side door. *Please*, Mr. Wentworth—you will do that for me?"

Wentworth jotted down the address and agreed to be there in half an hour. But his lips were twisted in a cynical smile, as he stepped away from the telephone. The setup was a trap, obviously—a very crudely baited trap, at that—having failed to kill him in three attempts his enemies intended to lure him out of the house for another try.

Yet he intended to keep that appointment. That girl, no matter who she might be, was a lead to the perpetrator of the atrocious massacre in St. Stephen's. And a lead was all that he asked....

Swiftly a plan began to take form in his brain.

"Jackson will drive me," he outlined it to his little council-of-war. "He will take up a position across the way from this tavern.

35

Nita, you can follow with Ram Singh—but you are not to get into any fracas that may occur, understand. If I need help, Jackson will be there to give it to me. You and Ram Singh are simply to keep watch—to follow us if anything should go wrong, and then go to Kirkpatrick."

Five minutes later Jackson drove out of the gateway and headed for Queens. At the corner of Forty-Seventh Street, Wentworth stopped him and proceeded the rest of the way on foot.

The Colonial Tavern was fairly large, with a bar in the front and a back room that opened onto the side street in the rear. Eight or ten men lounged at the bar, but at first glance the shadowy backroom seemed to be empty. Then he spied the girl in the booth beyond the door—and caught a glimpse of two men in a booth at the far corner.

That girl.... Wentworth's pulses leaped. She was the one who had driven the coupé that had picked up Fleming Trask the night before; the girl who had crouched fearfully over the wheel! But she did not seem to recognize him. Wentworth walked right up to her before she seemed to see him; stopped at the booth before she greeted him.

Then her eyes widened amazingly, and he realized that she was quite pretty. A girl of about twenty-two or three, with an oval face and a wealth of reddish-blonde hair. Her features were small and well formed, but it was her eyes that held his attention—big eyes that seemed to fill her whole face. She was striving hard to keep them from betraying her, he saw at once, but the fear that flared in their depths would not be denied.

She was playing a dangerous game, and she knew it….

"Mr. Wentworth—" she arose and extended her hand uncertainly—"oh, I am *so* glad you came. Please sit down. I shall try not to keep you too long, but what I have to say is so difficult—"

Wentworth sat down, and his eyes, now becoming accustomed to the half-gloom of the unlighted room, darted from booth to booth. Those two men in the corner booth… now he recognized one: Stump Fuller, one of Heinie Schneider's prize torpedoes. And that corner cubicle was not the only one that was occupied. There was a hard-looking customer in the booth directly opposite his own, another farther down the room. Yes, and still another in the telephone booth that commanded both the side doorway and the entrance to the barroom. Zeke Horowitz, another of the Schneider mob, he placed that last one.

At least five of them, and probably there were more out at the bar. This time, they were taking no chances—the trap was many-toothed. Now Wentworth could feel their cold eyes upon him, the deadly eyes of killers sizing up their prey while they waited for the signal to go into action. He turned back to the troubled blue eyes of the woman who had deliberately lured him there to his death.

CHAPTER 4
A TRAP CLOSES

THOSE EYES were fixed on Wentworth. They seemed to be trying to speak to him, trying to tell him something, trying to make a confidence the girl would not allow to pass her lips. Great, limpid pools, they were alive with fear, with concern, with anxiety—yes, with desperation.

"It is my father who is worrying me so much, Mr. Wentworth." She leaned over the little booth table toward him. "Perhaps you know of him—Melvin Gillespie? He is one of the foremost radio engineers in the country. Hundreds of radio inventions are his patents. Although he is over sixty, his mind is far more active than that of most much younger men—or at least it was until my brother Russell died."

She shuddered. "Since then, a change has come over him. He has been acting very peculiarly—moping and drawing more and more into himself. So much so that I became alarmed. Finally I persuaded him to permit Spencer Palmer, an old friend of our family, to psychoanalyze him in an attempt to dispel the morbidness that was settling over him."

Spencer Palmer… Wentworth's interest quickened at the mention of that name.

"For a while he seemed to improve under Dr. Palmer's treatment," the girl was saying. "He became more cheerful and began to take an interest in things. But it didn't last long. Now he's worse than ever. Sometimes, I catch his eyes studying me—and it makes me actually afraid of him. I'm afraid of what he may be planning to do. I don't—don't think he's quite sane, Mr. Wentworth."

Her voice was low, earnest, and her eyes fairly begged for understanding. But Wentworth caught those other cruel, cold eyes riveted on him; and he had only grudging admiration for her acting. She was stalling, waiting for something—something that would unleash that deadly pack of killers who now strained at their leashes....

"I don't really believe that my father had anything to do with that terrible slaughter in St. Stephen's church last night," her words caught his attention again. "But I do know that he hated Joab Robinson and Grace for breaking off Russell's engagement and sending him to his death. Father never forgave them for that, and I've been fearful of what brooding might do to him."

She trembled. "Last night he was *nowhere* near that church. He was at home working in his laboratory. But when the news of the tragedy came over the radio it shocked him terribly. He became as white as a sheet and dropped back into a chair. His lips kept moving, but I could not hear what he was saying. I couldn't catch anything but a mumble about *murder*—"

Murder—was that the signal? Wentworth had been watching those other booths from the corner of his eyes. Now he saw the men shifting to the edge of the benches, getting to their feet— saw the telephone booth opening. They were closing in for the kill... and she went right on with this Judas narrative!

"That's enough!" he told her grimly. "I know your game—and you've played it long enough. Look out!"

Her big eyes were suddenly stricken. The blood drained from her cheeks and she gasped faintly. But Wentworth had no more time for her. He had been busily planning every moment since he stepped into this back room. Now his plan went into swift, devastating action.

Suddenly, he appeared to slump in his seat, slipped beneath the table—but once he hit the floor he flashed into lightning-swift movement. This table, he had ascertained, was solid-topped, yet but lightly secured to the wall. His shoulders were under it now and as he heaved upright it tore loose with a cracking and snapping of splintered paneling. Now he had it in front of him, a shield protecting him from shoulders to below the knee.

Instantly bullets ripped into the table. He gripped it, flinging himself straight at his attackers—and from behind that table he loosed a stream of deadly accurate lead. The two killers in the corner, and the one at the back of the room, because of their position loomed as the most dangerous. Wentworth shot them down mercilessly.

This cleared the end of his room, freed his back, and Wentworth whirled to meet the others. Now the end of the table was down on the floor, shoving awkwardly forward like a mobile fortress. The thug who had been sitting in the booth across from him had deserted that hot spot and joined his mates in the barroom entrance.

Four remained now—Horowitz, from the telephone booth, and three others. They were crouching low, hugging the walls, creeping in to surround him—to get around his barricade and blast him out. Four guns rained lead upon him, splintering the table-top, ripping through it and crashing past his head.

Not much longer now… they were moving in closer… closer—then he sprang!

Like a hurricane-tossed rooftop, that table sailed across the room and caught Zeke Horowitz square in the face. His blood-curdling scream blended with the yell of terror that

came from the thug on Went-
worth's right as he gazed into the
automatic muzzle already blasting
him to hell. And then Wentworth's
lithe, bobbing, weaving figure was
across the room, was smashing his gun barrel down over the
skull of the killer who had thought to ambush him from the left.

One more remained there at the barroom entrance. Wentworth started toward him, but the fellow took to his heels, ran in
blind panic. That left only the girl. Wentworth turned to where
she cowered in a corner of the wrecked booth—and felt the hard
muzzle of a gun grind deep into his ribs.

"Drop it on the floor!" a tight, brittle voice rasped in his ear.
"Don't try to trick me. I'll shoot—and go scot-free, too, after
what you've pulled here. You're going outside—in a hurry."

"Oh, Carl—I thought you'd never come!" the girl gasped with
relief as she sprang from the booth and snatched up the gun
Wentworth had been forced to drop.

CARL? WENTWORTH caught a glimpse of his captor
as he was rushed to the side door. Now he recognized the grim-
faced man who had been the girl's companion the past night in
the coupé. A man of twenty-seven or twenty-eight, he judged—
square-jawed, high-cheekboned, with bushy eyebrows and a
crop of sandy hair. He did not seem to belong with the rest of
this routed killer pack, but there was no doubt about his seri-
ousness or that he meant exactly what he said. The gun barrel
never wavered from Wentworth's ribs. Hard fingers fastened in

41

his arm, rushed him through the doorway and into the coupé he had tried so desperately to board last night.

Where did this Carl fit in with Schneider's wolf-pack? Wentworth did not know, but it was plain neither he nor the girl was accustomed to the use of firearms. On a desperate gamble, Wentworth probably could have disarmed them both—but he much preferred to go for a little ride in that coupé....

It had taken Carl only a few seconds to get the upper hand and rush Wentworth out to the waiting machine. From first to last, the tavern battle had taken scarcely more than a very few minutes—so short a space that Jackson had not even had time to come to the rescue. Wentworth saw him running up the street, as the coupé door closed, saw him turn and dash back to where his car was parked.

Again the girl was at the wheel, her cheeks ashen and her fingers white-knuckled, as she gripped the wood and jammed her foot down on the throttle. The car left the curb with a leap, streaked down the street at top speed and swung around the first corner.

"Quite a business of kidnaping you two do, isn't it?" Wentworth remarked conversationally. "I admire the technique you are developing."

As he expected, the girl almost collapsed. Her mouth dropped open and she turned to stare at him as if he were the devil himself. But Carl did not bat an eye.

"That will be all from you," he snapped. "You will have all the chance you want to talk later—now shut up. If you don't...

well, I have also developed quite a technique in swinging this gun down on skulls!"

Wentworth grinned. He had gained his end—distracting their attention from his own car now creeping up behind them—he identified it in the rear-view mirror. Any moment now, Jackson would close up the gap and overhaul them.

But before Jackson could accomplish that, a big sedan hurtled past him and ate up the distance that separated it from the fleeing coupé. In a matter of seconds,  this strange car had flashed alongside, was crowding the coupé to the curb, up onto the sidewalk—and straight for an electric light pole! Too late Carl realized the danger… and was helpless to meet it.

"Look out, Joan!" he yelled, wide-eyed.

The girl screamed in terror, desperately fighting to swing clear of the pole. But in that instant Wentworth's arms wrapped around her and pulled her down beneath the door level, clear of the window. The moment he saw that oncoming machine he had spotted the tommy gun muzzle projecting from one of its windows… and knew what to expect.

The deadly chatter of that gangland typewriter seemed in their very ears; its bullets raked the interior of the coupé, front to rear—and then they crashed. First into a parcel post box that went clanging across the sidewalk, and then, at nearly forty miles an hour, into the unyielding light pole.

The coupé's bumper snapped and one of its fenders folded into an accordion, as it slammed into the pole, corkscrewing around it. Broken glass showered from the windshield. But now Wentworth had wedged his own body and the girl's tight against the seat, had himself braced for the shock—and they were not hurt by the collision.

Through the shattered windshield he glimpsed the murder car not twenty-five feet away. The doors opened as half a dozen thugs leaped out to finish their victims. But before they could reach the demolished coupé, Wentworth was out crouched in the wreckage—ready with the automatic he had snatched from Carl's unresisting hand.

Two of the killers went down before the leaden barrage of a tommy gun forced Wentworth to flatten out behind the inadequate barricade. Swiftly the others came in to finish him… But that was when Jackson suddenly took a hand in the game. With a squeal of brakes, his car pulled up beside the wreck—and his very first shot put the tommy-gunner out of action. Now Wentworth's other allies were on hand. Ram Singh swung his car in front of the gangster machine in an attempt to pocket it. Nita, at the window, was firing.

It was too much for the thugs. Their car backed up frantically, and Wentworth had a flashing glimpse of the driver. Angel McCabe—the Schneider lieutenant who had won an acquittal along with Jim Leary!

McCabe flung the rear door of the sedan open, and the three of his killers who were still on their feet raced to it and piled in pell-mell. With a snort of back firing gasoline the car got underway, whipped around in a circle and headed back toward New

York. But the moment McCabe's intention was clear, Wentworth sprinted to his own car and leaped in beside Jackson.

"Keep them in sight, Jackson," he ordered, as the car slipped into gear. "Never mind about traffic. Follow fast."

THOSE WERE large orders, for Angel McCabe drove like a madman. However, Jackson was his equal. In and out of traffic they snaked their way, disregarding red lights. Brakes squealed behind them as cursing drivers managed to avoid collisions by inches; police whistles shrilled indignant commands that were ignored. Like a fox fleeing from the hounds, Angel McCabe headed straight for the Manhattan that was his "native land" and employed every trick in his book to throw off that dogged pursuit.

Not until they reached the Queensborough Bridge did the gangster car come to a halt. Then a solid wedge of traffic blocked them, and there was no alternative but to wait. Wentworth and Jackson were not more than half a dozen cars behind, just as firmly welded into the traffic jam.

"We can hop out here and reach them before they move again," Jackson suggested, as he reached to set the emergency brake.

But Wentworth had already considered that course and rejected it. To creep up on McCabe would mean a gunfire showdown—nothing more. Even if they did down the gang lieutenant and his killers, they would be no closer to the solution of the Death Song murders, no nearer to pinning the guilt for that terrible St. Stephen's outrage onto the man who was responsible. McCabe was merely a pawn in this ruthless murder game; it was the king Wentworth wanted to reach.

Two cars behind them in the solid traffic, was what he needed to do it, a taxi-cab returning to Manhattan empty.

Angel McCabe and his companions
lay where they had fallen—slumped
in chairs, sprawled on the floor.

"Jackson," he said quickly, "hang onto their trail for about a mile—when you get on the other side of the bridge. Then let them give you the slip. It will give the cabbie a chance to follow them without being suspected."

By the time the traffic whistle blew again Wentworth was in the taxicab, and its driver knew that he was working for a five-dollar bonus if he kept his quarry in sight. Five dollars looked big to that hack man, and he did not intend to lose it. No matter how McCabe twisted and turned, the taxi trailed at a safe distance in his wake.

The chase came to an end at a hotel on upper Broadway in the seventies. McCabe ran the sedan into a nearby garage and led his men to the hotel entrance on foot. Wentworth strolled in a few minutes after them, even rode up in the same elevator. But *not* a Wentworth that any of them recognized—for he had been busy in that taxicab!

With his makeup kit on his lap, he had gone to work on his face, remodeling it so completely that the driver blinked in amazement when the transformed fare stepped out to pay him off. He had picked up a good looking young American, he would have sworn—"but this feller what got out, he looked more like a spick, so help me!"

Wentworth left the elevator at the same floor as the mobsters, but his destination was beyond theirs, at the far end of the corridor—until they had been admitted and an apartment door closed behind them. Then he retraced his footsteps swiftly, straight to the door that he had spotted in a small mirror held close to his shoulder.

Room 917. Already Wentworth had sketched the floor plan of the hotel. It was laid out in the form of an E, and Room 917 seemed to be the main entrance to a suite that occupied most of the end of one of the outside wings. For a moment he hesitated outside the door, listened; heard the low rumble of voices inside. Voices that he could not hope to distinguish or recognize. Somehow, he must get a look at that suite.

And then a possible way occurred to him.

Walking to the end of the corridor that ran through the central wing of the E, he stopped at the last door and pushed the button. No answer. Once more he tried—and then his skeleton key was slipping into the lock, clicked solidly and swung the mechanism. Warily he stepped into the room and closed the door behind him. The place was empty, evidently untenanted.

The shortest of the three wings, it did not reach out quite as far as the one in which Suite 917 was located. But when he parted the curtains carefully he found no difficulty in looking across the narrow intervening court into the opposite rooms. By now it was late afternoon. Shadows were deepening in the court, and lights were turned on in the suite that interested him. THE ROOM closest to his vantage point was most brightly lighted—and crowded. Half a dozen men sat around a table playing poker. Beyond that was another room where a single light burned at a desk. Angel McCabe stepped through the doorway of that room and joined the men at the poker table— and then a figure appeared at the window of the inner room and stared out at the sky. A thick-set man with graying hair and heavy jowls, who chewed restlessly on a cigar that had gone out between his lips.

James Leary—the man District Attorney Baker had vainly tried to convict of working hand-in-glove with Heinie Schneider's mob!

Wentworth's pulses leaped. There, before his eyes, was full confirmation of Stanley Kirkpatrick's suspicions. Fresh from a murderous attack on Wentworth's life, Angel McCabe and his killers had come straight back to their boss—Jim Leary!

There, across that narrow court, was the evidence needed to solve the St. Stephen's massacre, the murder of Leland Chaney, and the persistent attempts that had been made on his own life. There was the man responsible for this epidemic of lawlessness....

Wentworth's keen eyes were darting beyond the room in which Leary stood. The windows of that room were dark, yet it must be part of the same suite. A suite on the ninth floor, with only one floor intervening between it and the roof. That unlighted room was the answer!

Leary was still standing there at his window, nervously chewing on his cigar butt and impatiently glancing at his watch, when Wentworth drew back from the curtains and carefully let himself out of the room. There was nobody in the corridor, nobody to pass him as he reached the stairway and climbed up to the roof.

Carefully he picked his way across to the wing in which the Leary suite was located, and, as he did, his hands were busy beneath his opened vest—busy unwinding yards of thin, strong silken rope that had been wound around his body. The roof was edged with a low parapet, and there were plenty of poles and knobs to which this line could be made fast.

Cautiously he looked over the edge, selecting a place between the two darkened windows of that farthest room. It was out beyond the central wing of the E, which would be some protection from possible observation. The problem was to pass that upper floor without being seen, but that should not be difficult.

Already Wentworth had attached one end of the silken rope to a stout iron stanchion, the other around his waist. Then, keeping as flat against the building as possible, he let himself over—let himself down, hand over hand, foot by foot, until he was midway between the darkened windows. Then one hand pushed against the building, swung his body to the side—again, again, until he was swinging, in a gradually increasing arc, like a pendulum.

Wider and wider—until he was able to grasp the side of one of those darkened windows and cling there. He got a purchase for his knees on the sill, gently worked the window frame upward. The room was a bedroom. It was unoccupied. The door, between this and the room in which he had spotted Leary, was closed.

Noiselessly Wentworth stepped inside and detached the silken rope, the stout strand of the Spider's web that had so often proved an invaluable lifeline. Tiptoeing to the closed door, he listened.

Leary was still in that next room. He was talking to Angel McCabe.

"I don't like this," Wentworth heard Leary growl. "Five o'clock you said he'd be here—and it's ten after now. How did you know it was Heinie who called you, anyway? He was supposed to see me tonight—not at five. I'll give him five minutes more—then he can go to hell."

Five minutes and he would leave. But before he went, Jim Leary was scheduled for an interview he little expected....

IN THE bathroom that adjoined the bedroom, Wentworth went to work in front of a mirror—and his swiftly moving fingers performed uncanny miracles. Within a few short minutes he aged years. Deep lines and furrows came into his face; his skin grew sallow and wizened; his keen blue-gray eyes became watery and glistening. His lips disappeared entirely, and his teeth became hideous, discolored fangs. Over his brows went shaggy black ones that shaded his cavernous eyes; covering his head now a wig of tousled, matted, stringy black hair.

Out from the lining of his coat came a folded length of cloth that shook out into a long black cape—with it, a flowing black tie, a wide, floppy-brimmed black hat... and the Spider was ready.

Back to the door he scuttled, crouched close to the panel. Leary was still grumbling. McCabe was arguing with him. Then there was the sound of a door closing, and silence except for the restless shuffle of footsteps. McCabe had gone. Leary was alone—but only for a moment.

Soundlessly the bedroom door opened at his back—and when he whirled around from the window, it was to gape, open-mouthed, at a twisted, stooping figure that leered at him over the muzzle of a leveled automatic. This horrible, black-garbed figure came toward him, almost without moving; went past him to the door of the outer room and turned the key in the lock.

Not until then did that weird apparition make a sound, and then the noise which came from his throat was a low, half-mad cackle that sent chills dancing up Jim Leary's spine!

"Spider!" the name came almost soundlessly from his lips. "It's you—the Spider!"

"Yes, the Spider!" a cracked, jangling voice mocked him. "You ought to have known I would call on you sooner or later, Leary. You can't get away with wholesale murder—not even you, Jim Leary, who laughs at judges and district attorneys. When you murder a church full of people your case passes from the jury into my hands!"

Leary's face blanched and his big body trembled as he lowered himself heavily into a chair.

"I didn't do that, Spider," he husked. "I didn't have anything to do with that, so help me God!"

"And you didn't have anything to do with Heinie Schneider and the racket drive on the loan companies!" that nerve-racking voice mocked him. "You were innocent of all the nasty charges the district attorney brought against you—weren't you, Leary?"

The automatic raised ever so slightly, pointed straight at Leary's ample belly. The finger on the trigger moved, whitening the knuckle.

"All right—I admit that!" Leary gasped, while his face became wet with perspiration. "I admit he had the goods on me, even if he couldn't prove it. But that's all, Spider. I'm no bloody murderer—"

Those glittering eyes almost laughed at him.

"Maybe there were some killings—necessary killings," Leary blurted in utter desperation, "but nothing like that church slaughter. I'm no butcher, Spider—I don't go in for murdering women and kids."

"Or for killing a terrified man who was trapped helplessly in his own room?" the mocking voice suggested.

"I know—you mean Chaney," Leary gulped. "But I don't know a thing about it. Somebody got in there ahead of me—before I could even get to Chaney." Some of the terror went out of his eyes, to be replaced by puzzlement—then a kindling spark of anger. "I don't know who did that, Spider," he repeated earnestly, "but when I find out who it was—"

Suddenly Wentworth tensed. The automatic rose warningly, and the words died on Leary's lips—faded into a half-gasp... for now he, too, had heard. Like one who expects to face his doom, Leary's eyes swiveled to the locked door of that outer room.

Through the paneling came the sound of weird music... the baleful melody of the Song of Death!

Like a stricken man, Leary sat there, quaking in his chair. But Wentworth leaped past him and sprang to the door. His fingers grasped the key, tugged at it frantically when it stuck in the lock—but already he knew that he was too late. Already the mad howling in that outer room told him what he would find.

Angel McCabe and his six companions lay where they had fallen—on the floor, slumped in their chairs, sprawled over the table—seven men who had died in an agony that was stamped indelibly on their contorted faces!

Wentworth knew that there was no use trying to revive them, no use listening for a heart-beat in those stilled breasts. Like the wedding guests in St. Stephen's, their lives had been winked out in a moment of awful madness. And, as in the case of Leland Chaney, the room offered not the slightest evidence of how they had met their fate.

His eyes flashed from the bodies to the walls, the windows, and the doorway to the hall—when suddenly the door behind him slammed shut. Before he could leap to it, he heard the click of the lock. But that door was not constructed to resist the impact of a charging body. The lock snapped and it flung wide— to reveal an empty room beyond. Leary was gone.

Quickly Wentworth ran into the bedroom. Another door there disclosed how the politician had flown. He had escaped into the hallway—and now Wentworth caught the echo of his wildly bellowing voice.

"The Spider! The Spider!" he howled as he fled.

In a flash Wentworth was across the room and had yanked the door open, but Leary's uproar had already brought results. Half a dozen wide-eyed people were out there in the corridor—to stand transfixed when the fearsome visage of the Spider peered out at them.

To attempt to escape that way would be to invite disaster and to leave a trail of witnesses behind him. Yet there was no time to lose; the police would arrive at any minute.

Wentworth turned back into the room, locked the door.

Swiftly he stepped to the window and untied the silk rope, which he had secured to the curtain tie-back. Fastening it around his waist, he stepped out onto the ledge and lowered the window behind him before he swung out into space—and worked his way, hand over hand, upward.

The moment he reached the roof he stripped off his cape and hat, tore at the telltale Spider make-up and restored the guise of an elderly Cuban in which he had entered the hotel. He had scarcely finished when the roof door opened and four men came charging out. Instantly they spied the black cape lying over the parapet and ran to it—and just as quickly Wentworth slipped through the doorway, to close and lock it behind him.

By the time he reached the ninth floor, the corridor was thronged with excited tenants who milled around the policemen now barring them from the doorway of 917. A dozen men and women were trying to speak at once, but through the pandemonium he caught the damning testimony of those who had glimpsed him at the bedroom door.

"It was the Spider, all right," one old man declared shakily. "I saw him with my own eyes. He was glaring out of that doorway, and had a pistol in his hand. I don't know how I'm still alive—after the way he killed that roomful of men without giving them a chance!"

The Spider was guilty in their eyes; guilty of committing the Song of Death murders. For there, in the hands of the sergeant at the doorway, was one of those skull noted sheets of music paper that Wentworth must have overlooked in the death room....

CHAPTER 5
TALE OF TERROR

R ICHARD WENTWORTH had implored Nita to take no part in any trouble that might result from his rendezvous in the Woodside tavern. But when she had seen him hemmed in by killers she completely disregarded orders. The fierce-eyed Sikh was at her side as she plunged into the mêlée.

Eagerly Ram Singh leaped from their car, his long, keen-bladed knife clutched in his brown hand. The fight was too short; that was Ram Singh's only regret. Only one of the killers felt a taste of that razor-edged blade—a thug intent upon sending a treacherous slug into Wentworth's back. The blood spurted from his severed jugular before he could pull the trigger. Then the battle was over, the enemy had flown.

Nita's voice reminded Ram Singh that there still remained work to be done.

"Give me a hand with this man," she called from the door of the wrecked coupé. "He is badly hurt—and the police will be here any moment."

Single-handed, the Sikh lifted the wounded man from the demolished car and ran with him to where Nita was helping a dazed girl into the sedan. Then he sprang back behind the wheel and got the car under way.

Fearfully Joan Gillespie looked up into Nita's eyes, tried to stammer a question. But Nita understood without words.

"I know," she reassured soothingly.

"You are Joan Gillespie, aren't you? And this is—?"

"Carl—Carl Winkler," the girl answered automatically. "He is my father's assistant. We are—are engaged. But I don't understand… Where are we going? Why are we running away?"

"We are hurrying Carl to a doctor," Nita told her. "He probably is not seriously injured, but must have medical attention immediately. If we waited here for the police, there would be delay—questions. You didn't want to wait for the police, did you, Joan?"

Suddenly the girl's big blue eyes widened with terror, and her arm tightened around Carl Winkler's unconscious shoulders.

"No—not the police!" she sobbed. "We've had *so* much trouble already. All that shooting in the tavern—and then that terrible smash-up! I was afraid of this, when we started. But Carl insisted—he said it was the only way."

Then she seemed to realize that she was speaking too freely. A guilty flush spread over her cheeks and her lower lip caught between her teeth. Not another word came from her, as the car crossed the bridge and headed uptown to the private hospital run by Dr. Rogers. This physician served Richard Wentworth to the limit of his ability—but even then considered whatever he might do poor enough compensation for the invaluable services he, himself, had received.

Here Winkler was examined, had his wounds dressed and was put to bed. Up to that point the girl had clung desperately to her composure. But when it was established that Winkler was not dangerously wounded, that he needed only care and rest to recover, her self control snapped. She gave way to tempestuous tears.

Nita let her cry it out until the storm of hysteria was past.

"Now suppose you tell me about it," she urged. "I am Nita van Sloan, Richard Wentworth's fiancée. I know why he came to meet you today. But I don't know why you lured him into that trap. What is it all about, Joan? I know you are in trouble—perhaps two women's heads will be better able to solve your problem than one."

"I didn't know it would be anything like that—I swear I didn't, Miss van Sloan," the girl said brokenly. "I don't know a thing about those men in the tavern. I thought they were just customers—until they began shooting. Carl was the only one who was supposed to be there—just Carl and me. We were going to—were going to force Mr. Wentworth to come with us."

"Why, Joan?" Nita prompted gently.

"Because we have been so worried about father," Joan Gillespie lifted haggard eyes, and then repeated the story she had told Wentworth. "We have been trying our best to help him, protect him," she finished. "Exactly what it is we are trying to protect him against, I do not know. I think that Carl knows—and that is what frightens me. Because, if he *does* know it must be something so terrible that he does not dare let me know the truth!"

"Why do you think that, Joan?" Nita followed up. "And you haven't told me yet why you wanted to kidnap Dick."

"It was because of last night," Joan explained. "This will answer both your questions. I told you how queerly father acted when he heard the news of the St. Stephen's tragedy. I told Carl about that, when he came in an hour or so later. The moment he heard it he became almost as excited as father. He said that

59

he must go to the church right away, and wanted to borrow my car. I insisted on going along with him."

She went on. "When we reached the church… well, we saw Mr. Wentworth there. He… he came running after us with the police and tried to stop us. They shot at us, and Mr. Wentworth tried to get into the car… but Carl forced him off the running board. I did not know who Mr. Wentworth was, but Carl did. Carl knew all about him and was afraid that he would make trouble for us with the police and trouble for father. So we decided to make him come with us today, and force him to listen. I know that sounds silly now, but it is why we did it."

The girl seemed sincere. Her story was jumbled, but that was only natural after what she had been through.

"No matter how it sounds, I believe you, Joan," Nita declared. "I want to help you. Suppose you take me home with you and introduce me to your father? Perhaps, if I talk to him, I can induce him to tell me what is troubling him, or what he fears."

Joan Gillespie agreed eagerly, but the moment they drew up in front of the large, old-fashioned house in Woodside, Nita sensed that she was doomed to failure. As she stepped out of the car she caught a glimpse of a face peering out of one of the lower windows—a face that stared at the car with wild, frightened eyes. It was there for a moment, and then vanished.

MELVIN GILLESPIE met them in the hallway. He was tall, sparely built, with the expressive features of a Shakespearian tragedian rather than those which might have been expected of a prosaic radio engineer. He smiled an acknowledgment of the introduction, but Nita could read the thinly veiled suspicion only half concealed in the depths of his troubled eyes.

"Miss van Sloan… van Sloan…" he repeated meditatively.

"You read her name in the papers this morning, father," Joan tried to refresh his memory. "She was one of the few who escaped from St. Stephen's church last night."

The effect of that announcement was profound, devastating. Every bit of color ebbed from Melvin Gillespie's face, leaving his cheeks a ghastly bluish white, and his lips a tight, bloodless line. But it was his eyes that fascinated Nita. All hell seemed suddenly let loose in them—the wild eyes of a soul-tortured maniac!

"What is it, father? What is the matter?" Joan screamed, and she ran forward, clasped him in her arms. "Please tell me! I can't stand to see you look like that!"

But Gillespie had now regained something of his control.

"Nothing, Joan, nothing at all," he said in a trembling voice that belied his words. "You are simply upset, imagining things. I think perhaps you had better lie down for a while, you look tired, my dear."

His eyes lifted from his daughter's bowed head to Nita—eyes now coldly polite but plain in their suggestion. He wanted her to go—and she knew that there would be little use remaining any longer. Melvin Gillespie knew something about that ghastly slaughter in St. Stephen's, something that was eating at him like a virulent cancer—but his lips were determinedly sealed.

"If there is anything I can do… for either of you…" she made a valiant effort to pierce his icy shell.

But he shook his head. "Thank you, but I think we can manage very well—alone." His dismissal was uncompromising.

Nita had reached the door before Joan came running, to follow her out onto the porch.

"I'm sorry," she apologized, "but you see how he is. It seems there is nothing we can do—nothing but watch him going crazy!"

"It may not be as bad as that," Nita tried to calm her. "But I want you to let me know if he gets any worse... if anything happens or if there is anything that I can do."

With the girl's fervent promise, she went back to the car, and felt those agitated, terror-haunted eyes once more boring into her; could almost see the relief on Melvin Gillespie's face now that she was gone.

WHEN HE heard the Death Song killings of Angel McCabe and his six companions laid at the door of the Spider, Richard Wentworth faced a serious problem. This evidence might be all needed to make Stanley Kirkpatrick carry out his threat to clap him into jail on the testimony of the two officers who had seen him fleeing from St. Stephen's church after the bombing. On the other hand, to take flight now would give the commissioner seeming proof that Richard Wentworth *was* the Spider, and that the Spider was guilty of this outrageous charge....

Wentworth finally solved his dilemma by going home to Sutton Place. Nita waited there to tell him of her experience with Joan Gillespie and her father.

Nothing happened that night, but in the morning the newspaper headlines shrieked the news of the Spider's guilt. One after the other, Wentworth scanned their accounts—read the lurid testimony of those excited "eye witnesses," including the four who had "almost trapped" the Spider on the hotel roof. The murder stage, he learned, had been set in the suite rented by Benjamin Karpen, who was among the victims.

Of James Leary there was no mention whatever. The crafty politician was far too careful for that. Next time, Wentworth vowed, Leary would not slip out so easily—and that next time must come in the very near future. In a desperate attempt to cover his own guilt, Leary had declared war on the Spider—and now the Spider would take his trail!

However, before there was an opportunity to begin that hunt, other things intervened.

The death of Angel McCabe and his pals was not the only news of what the tabloids had euphoniously labeled the "Melody Murders." Sharing the front page with it were the stories of two more loan company executives who had died with the Song of Death in their ears and a sheet of music paper, with the death's head tune, in their possession.

Wilbur Barlow, of the Greater New York Family Loan, had fled from his Park Avenue apartment to a Westchester hideaway—and had died there, alone and far from his friends. Theodore Conboy, of the Personal Bond Corporation, had laughed at the threat and gone through with a nightclub dinner party he had planned—only to condemn fifteen other men and women to death with him!

The Song of Death was inescapable, infallible; once the grisly warning notice made its appearance, the victim's fate was sealed.

That was the grim message between the lines—and Wentworth visualized the terror it must be breeding throughout the city. Whoever was wielding this threatening club was forging a weapon too soon to be invincible; a weapon that would not only shatter the last thought of resistance among the loan company people but also would be brandished over the head of whatever industry the racketeers might next choose for their attention....

The newspapers were still in Wentworth's lap, when the telephone rang. As he expected, it was Stanley Kirkpatrick. The commissioner wanted to have a talk with him—at headquarters.

"All right, Kirk, be there in half an hour," he agreed. A bleak half smile hovered around the corners of his mouth as he dropped the instrument back into its cradle.

This was according to schedule—only about twelve hours later than he had expected it. Those twelve hours must mean that Kirkpatrick had held off until he felt sure of his course. Now he must be ready.

Again the telephone demanded Wentworth's attention.

This time it was a feverishly excited, terror-stricken voice that babbled over the wire. John Doremus, a wealthy Wall Street broker, whose huge fortune was attributed to his iron nerve in times of crisis. Now seemingly that iron nerve had melted; Doremus was thoroughly scared.

"They're after me, Dick!" he quavered. "Those devils who are running this Death Song racket. Yesterday they called me twice and demanded money. First a hundred thousand, and then two hundred thousand because I didn't agree the first time. I tried to have the call traced, but it was from a dial pay booth. This morning I got the death notice—one of those sheets of skeleton head music. I found it under my door as I started to leave the house."

He begged, "What will I do Dick? I'm afraid any moment I'll hear that hellish music. My people are sure that nobody has had a chance to get into the house, but that doesn't seem to mean anything!"

Into Wentworth's mind flashed the memory of Leland Chaney trapped and murdered in his locked room; and there before him in the newspaper was the reminder of how Barlow and Conboy had met their fate—indoors.

"Get out of that house immediately, Jack," he gave his swift directions. "Don't go near your office. Come down here to Sutton Place in your own car without delay. You will be safe here, but God knows where else."

John Doremus could not obey fast enough. Two servants acting as guards, got into the rear of the limousine with him, while another rode in front beside the chauffeur. Less than five minutes to Sutton Place, and he would be safe....

WENTWORTH WAS waiting for him. Standing at a third floor window of the Sutton Place stronghold, he was watching the side street down which Doremus's car would come—when suddenly there was a tremendous crash on the opposite corner! A limousine, turning into the side street from Sutton Place, apparently had gotten out of control—had cut across the street in a wide arc and crashed, head-on, into the corner building!

One glance at that limousine through a pair of binoculars was sufficient to identify it. John Doremus'!

Wentworth got out onto the street in record time. He reached the wrecked machine before the gathering spectators had had presence of mind to do more than stand and gape at the dead man who lay over the wheel, the stunned one who fell against the jammed door as he tried to tug it open.

In a moment Wentworth had that door yanked open, was helping the fellow out into the street. Then he opened the rear door, and looked in at three bodies that lay in a tangled heap on the floor. Of the five who had ridden in that car, only the man beside the chauffeur had escaped the fate that overtook them when they had almost reached safety.

"What happened?" Wentworth asked. He shook the man, repeated his question in a louder voice.

The fellow cupped his left ear in the familiar manner of those who are hard of hearing.

"What happened? Tell me about it!" Wentworth fairly yelled.

"I don't know," the dazed man shrugged hopelessly. "The master was afraid. We were all afraid. That was why he brought us along. We were watching for any sign of an enemy—and then I heard music back in the car. I thought the master had turned on the radio. But when I looked at Mallory, he was the chauffeur, his face was all twisted as if he had convulsions. He screamed something. Then he fell over the wheel, and he drove straight into that building."

The Song of Death! It had sounded its knell right there in the limousine—and the only one to escape was this half deaf servant!

Wentworth climbed in over the huddled bodies and went to work on that rear compartment. With his pocketknife he slitted the upholstery, the side walls, the wall behind the chauffeur—and there, embedded in the framework of the coach body, was an amplifier connected to a skillfully concealed antenna. A compact arrangement that had almost escaped his searching scrutiny.

He was examining it when wailing sirens warned him of the arrival of the police. They pushed the crowd back from the death car, and a sergeant ordered Wentworth out—just as another car pulled up containing the captain of the precinct. His eyes bulged in amazement when he beheld the corpse-filled car—and Wentworth climbing out of it.

"The commissioner sent me for you, Mr. Wentworth," he explained, "to offer my car to take you down to headquarters. But this—"

"Never mind about this, McCarthy," Wentworth dismissed. "There is nothing more you can do for them—the Song of Death has finished the job. Let's get on down to see the commissioner."

So Stanley Kirkpatrick had sent for him in order that there would be no doubt about his appearing at headquarters… Not an arrest, of course; just an escort… But when Wentworth stepped into the office he did not blame the harassed commissioner. Stanley Kirkpatrick's face was drawn and haggard. His eyes were red, swollen—those of a man who has had little sleep for forty-eight hours.

"MORE BAD news for you, Kirk," Wentworth greeted, as he dropped into the chair beside the commissioner's desk. "John Doremus is the latest Song of Death victim," and then he told what he knew of the broker's passing.

"I just had a flash on it," Kirkpatrick nodded wearily. "There seems to be one right after the other. Three already this morning. This is the sort of thing that breeds wild panic, Dick—death that strikes from nowhere and seems to be inescapable. You see what is happening already—you've read this morning's papers?"

He leaned forward and looked searchingly into Wentworth's eyes. "But I wonder if you had to read those papers, Dick? I wonder if you don't know far more about this than they have printed? About the death of Angel McCabe and his gang, for example. The Spider was there in the Monitor Hotel yesterday; I know that. Perhaps his presence there at that time was just a coincidence—and perhaps he has learned the secret of the Song of Death operation and was giving Leary and Schneider a dose of their own medicine?"

The commissioner was watching like a hawk, waiting for him to make a slip; some admission that would be tantamount to a confession of knowledge which he was holding back from the police. But Wentworth had fenced with Kirkpatrick before.

"Perhaps the Spider could answer that," he admitted smiling. "But, as far as I am concerned, at present I am a lot more interested in finding out who planted that amplifier in John Doremus' car and who sent the music over it that killed him and his servants."

"This is a time when I need your cooperation, Dick," Kirkpatrick pleaded. "If there is anything more that you know—"

He seemed to realize already that he was getting nowhere, and the ringing of his telephone came as a welcome interruption. He clapped it to his ear, listened, and the haggard lines grooved even more deeply into his face.

"That was from the criminal court," he said wearily as he put back the receiver. "Judge Delaney has just suspended sentence on Heinie Schneider and Ohlau and Goodman!"

"*Suspended sentence!*" Wentworth almost leaped from his chair.

That was impossible! Schneider and his henchmen had been convicted by overwhelming evidence. There was no possible question of their guilt; no remotest vestige of doubt or of anything that might be construed as extenuating circumstances. But, nevertheless, it was true.

Five minutes later one of Kirkpatrick's lieutenants came in and confirmed the incredible news.

"The judge was scared," he spat bitterly, "scared out of his pants. He was as white as a sheet when he took the bench—and he freed those killers because he knew that death was hanging over his own head. He knew that his life wouldn't be worth a damn if he sent them up!"

CHAPTER 6
VENGEANCE IS MINE!

"THERE YOU have the reason for this reign of terror!" Stanley Kirkpatrick thumped his fist down on his desk. "I knew from the start that Jim Leary was behind it. Starting with that fiendish, spectacular murder in St. Stephen's, these killings have all been designed to spread such terror that Schneider and his thugs would be turned loose. More than that—this outrageous display of gang power will serve as a warning to any other loan company men who might be inclined to oppose the racket when it clamps down on them. It means racket rule for New York, Dick—and how in God's name can we fight them, when even a hard won conviction means nothing but a suspended sentence?"

Wentworth was inclined to agree, in the main, with that dismal analysis and prophecy. Undoubtedly Schneider and his lieutenants had been liberated because of the terror the Song of Death killings had aroused. But there were angles to those murders which did not quite fit in with Kirkpatrick's theory.

John Doremus, for example. Doremus had had no connection whatever with the personal loan business, yet he had been marked for death... And Melvin Gillespie... What was he—another threatened victim, or merely a tool of the Leary-Schneider mob?

Wentworth had tried to reach Gillespie by telephone twice since Nita had narrated her experience, but the old man and his daughter both seemed to have disappeared from their home. The servant who answered professed to know nothing of their whereabouts or when they would return. That seemed particularly strange after the promise Joan Gillespie had given Nita....

"This ghastly threat of inexplicable death leaves us absolutely helpless," the police commissioner repeated. "How can we expect witnesses to testify in the face of such a threat? If a judge can be intimidated, what hope is there for juries, prosecutors—"

Suddenly he stopped, and his fingers brushed agitatedly at his mustache in that telltale indication of grave concern. His eyes turned to Wentworth—thoughtful eyes that were filling with apprehension.

"You remember, Schneider made several veiled threats against the district attorney during the trial," he recalled. "One wasn't so veiled—it was an out-and-out threat against his life. And now Schneider is free. That means that Kenneth Baker is in very real danger, Dick—he and every man who helped him build up his case. I am convinced that St. Stephen's slaughter was staged primarily to get Baker. They failed that time, but next—"

Without waiting to complete his sentence, he reached for the telephone and asked for the district attorney's office. For long moments he held the line, while the uneasiness in his eyes increased.

"There doesn't seem to be any reply from the district attorney's office," the doubtful voice of the puzzled operator came at last. "I have tried all their lines. None of them answer. But I have one open line that I am holding—a party who is waiting to speak to Assistant Newton. He was to be called to the phone, but he doesn't seem to answer—"

"Cut me in on that line!" Kirkpatrick clipped… and instantly the color drained from his ruddy cheeks.

For over that line came a weird melody that he knew unquestionably was the fatal Song of Death!

Wentworth caught it, too; caught the wild bedlam of madhouse yells that drowned it out—and he raced Kirkpatrick for the door. Even as they sprinted down the street to the building that housed the New York County District Attorney's staff, they felt that they would be too late. They found the door locked

71

when they pounded up to the prosecutors' office. Kirkpatrick put his fist through the glass upper half—then stood framed in the sharply studded orifice, staring in on a scene of gruesome horror.

It was Wentworth who reached inside and turned the latch; he who led the way into that shambles, picking a path between the bodies that littered the floor. Death was on every side of them—wherever they looked! From office to office they stalked—but death had been to each cubicle before them!

District Attorney Kenneth Baker and his whole staff were dead—and there, beneath a paper weight at one side of Baker's desk, was a sheet of music paper that was studded with grinning skeleton heads instead of notes!

Stanley Kirkpatrick was stunned by that wholesale slaughter that had robbed Manhattan of its entire corps of prosecutors. But he was soon to learn that this was only the beginning. Before evening six other witnesses, who had testified for the state during the racket trial, met their death—and a dozen others, trembling and begging for protection, were besieging his office with the death warnings they had received. Mocking warnings of a fate against which he knew that he could offer no protection!

Justice was prostrate—and Stanley Kirkpatrick, writhing in his impotence, did not dare look those doomed victims in the eye....

ALL THAT afternoon Richard Wentworth had tried in every possible way to locate James Leary. All of the Broadway café and hotel bars where the politician was almost a fixture he visited; all of the bookies with whom he was a regular customer, the haunts where he was to be found nearly every day. But Leary was in none of them. Nobody had seen him since shortly after the jury had turned him free.

Leary had disappeared… but that evening Wentworth netted a prize almost as much to his liking.

His quest had taken him to a side street hotel in the Times Square district that had figured in the trial as one of Leary's hangouts. Wentworth had traversed the long lobby that ran through from one street to the other, and was just stepping into the taproom, when a familiar-looking figure erupted from a phone booth and swaggered to the street.

Heinie Schneider!

Wentworth was after him in a flash, trailing him to a West Forty-fifth Street barroom, where he was joined by three of his mobsters. Three dangerous killers, Wentworth identified them. For five minutes they lingered at the bar, while Heinie talked and they listened, their eyes narrow-slitted, their heads nodding understanding. Then they were ready. Schneider led the way, and Wentworth now trailed them to an office building on East Forty-Second Street near Madison Avenue.

Once he knew their destination, he gave them ample time to go up on the elevator, then stepped into the lobby and ran his eyes down the directory of tenants. Home Finance Association—that white-lettered name fairly leaped out at him from the black background! Heinie Schneider was losing no time cashing in on the wave of terror that was deluging the city. Brazenly and openly, he was marching in on his victims, backed by the guns of his deadliest killers!

Again Wentworth scrutinized the directory, until he located a firm with offices on the top floor of the building. He made a note of the name. When he stepped into the elevator, he had two fellow passengers—two men who were badly frightened if he knew the telltale signs of fear. They got off on the fourth floor—the floor that was occupied entirely by the Home Finance Association. When the door opened, Wentworth saw more than a dozen men standing around in little groups in the wide reception room that faced the elevator.

"Quite a crowd in there tonight, isn't there?" he remarked as the car resumed its trip.

"Yeah, they're holding some sorta meeting." The operator nodded.

A meeting? This then was something bigger than the ordinary marching in on a victim and giving him his orders. Those men in the elevator had been loan company men. Executives, probably. And they were there to attend a meeting—a meeting over which Heinie Schneider and his killers would preside….

Somehow, Wentworth knew, he had to attend that meeting. But how?

On the top floor he found his answer. That floor was silent and deserted. Then the door of the freight elevator, at the rear of the corridor, opened and a dungaree-clad porter stepped out to take aboard the bags of waste the cleaning-woman had stacked beside the shaft. The porter went about his business and paid no attention to the stranger who was roaming down the corridor looking at the names on the office doors; paid no attention until the stranger had reached the elevator… and then it was too late.

Wentworth was on top of him in a flash. Pinning the porter's arms behind him, he dumped the fellow on his stomach and jabbed a gun muzzle into the back of his neck.

"Take it easy and nothing will happen to you," he warned. "All I want is your clothes. Take them off. I'll only use them a few minutes—and there's a double sawbuck for your trouble."

Wide-eyed, the Italian stripped off his dungarees and shirt—stuffing the twenty-dollar bill into the top of his shoe. With no attempt at resistance, he allowed himself to be gagged and tied up with a length of rope that was in the car. Then with the porter lying on the elevator floor, beneath a covering of waste filled bags, Wentworth got into the man's clothing and went to work on his own face with a makeup kit.

At last he was ready. The car started down, floor after floor, to the fourth. When he opened the door, he found this part of the floor deserted, but the hum of voices came plainly from farther front. Cautiously he walked forward. Now the reception room was empty, but the voices came from a large room at its rear—a sort of meeting room, he found, when he put his eye to the keyhole.

NEARLY TWENTY men were in there gathered around a nervous little man who stood behind a table. He was so badly frightened that his teeth almost chattered as he addressed them.

"—and so as chairman of this committee, representing the personal finance companies of this city, I can only advise you to make peace with Mr. Schneider and his organization," he was saying. "Further... er... conflict will only ruin our business entirely. Already people are afraid to come to us. If we meet Mr. Schneider's terms, we can readjust our rates and bonuses—"

A committee of bankers representing the entire personal finance industry in New York! Schneider had indeed been working fast! In that room he was about to undo all that the murdered district attorney had accomplished—welding the shackles firmly on these men who had dared to oppose him. The district attorney was gone; the courts were intimidated; the police were helpless. Now nothing stood in Heinie Schneider's way—nothing but the Spider!

Wentworth hurried back down the corridor. He stripped off the porter's clothing, donned a flowing black cape and tie. He transformed his face with lightning-fast fingers, slipped on the tousled black wig, the floppy black hat. Then he sped back to the meeting room door.

Now one of the other men in that room was upon his feet.

"If we yield to these outrageous demands, we might as well close up shop and go out of business," he flayed his fellows. "You know well enough that the law will not allow us to charge interest sufficiently high to repay such extortion. I realize," his voice was bitter, "that it's suicide for us either way. But I'd rather do it quickly—"

"All right, if that's the way you want it, Jonas!" Schneider's voice whipped at him, and the gangster and his bullies loomed behind the table. "You been makin' trouble from the start. Now—"

He nodded—and his killers went into action.

The man Jonas died with three slugs of lead tearing through

his body. Then the murderous thugs turned to others on the committee marked by Schneider for elimination. But before they could press triggers a second time, the door of that meeting room flung open and a weird apparition scuttled through it. A twisted, stooping figure that glared at them with glittering eyes while a mad, jangling cackle of sound burst from his lipless mouth!

Jaws sagging, gun-hands muscle-bound, those cold-blooded killers stood there and quailed in the face of the death they had dealt so wantonly. With horrified eyes they gaped into the blazing muzzles of the twin automatics that filled the room with thunderous doom.

"The Spider! That's the Spider!" Schneider howled. "Get him, you rats!"

Two of his killers never heard his words—because they died. The third triggered his weapon desperately, but that dancing phantom offered no target. The gunman's bullets went wild—and then a black hole sprouted squarely between his eyes. Now Heinie Schneider shrieked wildly and dropped to his knees. Frantically he tried to get back onto his feet, while whimpering curses mingled with the hysterical pleas that dribbled from his lips. But Wentworth's lead slammed him back mercilessly and flung him, a limp, bullet-riddled heap, at the feet of the men he had thought to victimize.

Wild pandemonium swept that room. Too frightened to move while death scythed through the air all around them, the loan bankers broke madly the moment Schneider fell. Almost instantly, the room was empty—except for the black, stooped vengeance that hovered over the sprawled bodies of the gangsters. For an instant he bent over each—long enough to press the bottom of a small cigarette lighter against the dead forehead.

And in each spot where that lighter pressed, the image of a crimson spider bloomed—an indelible spider that was a challenge and a warning to Jim Leary and all the underworld that the justice they had mocked and scorned had not altogether failed!

HIS TASK finished, Wentworth retreated swiftly to the freight elevator, stripped off his make-up and got back into the porter's outfit. When the police swarmed into the building he was busily wheeling out his cinder barrels—to stand gaping blankly at an excitement about which he seemingly knew nothing. Then he found the opportunity to slip into the swiftly gathering crowd….

He was free now.

In a nearby bar he got rid of the dungarees and made himself presentable. Yet, as he headed back to Sutton Place, he was more puzzled than ever. A death's head music sheet warning would have reduced those panicky committeemen to abject terror—and yet Schneider had made no attempt to use that threat. Instead, he had risked coming there and addressing them personally. Why?

More than ever Wentworth sensed that Schneider and Leary were not alone in this savage campaign of death and outlawry. Something behind them was far more powerful and terrible than they… The death of Schneider and his killers would, he hoped, in some measure check the unreasoning terror that had gripped the city—but what effect would those executions have upon this someone who was behind the mobsters?

Wentworth wondered… and when he reached home the answer seemed to be waiting there for him.

Nita met him anxiously the moment he stepped out of the elevator and into his luxurious, third floor living room.

"I have been so worried about you, Dick," she whispered as he took her in his arms and kissed her. "It was foolish, I suppose, but knowing that the telephone was out of order I could not help imagining that you might be trying to call us."

"The telephone?" Wentworth's brows lifted.

"We didn't know about it ourselves," Nita told him. "It seems there has been considerable trouble with all the phones along this street. Two emergency repair men were here. They left only a few minutes ago."

Emergency repair men… Again that tingling warning rang in Wentworth's brain—and into his mind flashed a vision of that deadly amplifier and antenna he had found in John Doremus' car!

"Where were they working, Nita—*quick!*"

"Why, over there at the window and in your study." Nita was taken aback. But before she could question him, he was across the room, was hunting feverishly for new wiring.

Carefully tucked away beneath the cushion of a window-seat he found what he sought—a length of wire that had no connection with the telephone; a wire that led to a minute amplifier hidden beneath a drape at the foot of the seat. Even as he grabbed it and started to rip it free, the opening bars of the Song of Death came floating eerily into the room!

"Downstairs!" Wentworth yelled, as he led the way to the stairs. "They have planted more than one of these devilish things!"

In a moment the third floor was deserted, and they were hurrying to a storeroom that was kept stocked with an extraneous accumulation of supplies designed to meet any emergency. Under Wentworth's direction, they stuffed their ears with cotton and then donned flying helmets as an added protection. Not until they could scarcely hear one another shout did they dare return to the upper floor to locate two more amplifiers. Two more death broadcasters that, a few minutes sooner, would have chained them with the spell of madness until doom encompassed them....

CHAPTER 7
CHAINS OF FEAR

THOSE CONCEALED amplifiers were the means of broadcasting the Song of Death; there could be no question about that. From somewhere in the city that diabolical composition was being sent out onto the ether to be picked up by these specially tuned receivers… but how a tune possibly could kill a man was something wholly beyond Richard Wentworth's comprehension. He had heard of madness being induced by the constant repetition of a succession of sounds over a great length of time. But the effect of this melody was almost instantaneous—and not only maddening but deadly.

This sinister problem was beyond the sphere of the ordinary physician. It belonged, more properly, to the psychiatrist—which was why Wentworth paid a visit to Spencer Palmer the next morning.

Palmer listened carefully, sitting with his elbows on the arms of his chair, fingertips of both hands gently touching in front of him. It was a little while before he ventured a reply.

"The human brain is a very delicate mechanism," was what he said. "One about which we realize that we know very little. We know, for example, that the radio waves which fill the air have a very definite effect on some delicately tuned brains. Just how far that effect goes we have not been able to determine."

He went on. "We know that a person can be conditioned to hypnosis by radio. We know that even the temperature of the human body can be raised by radio currents passing through it. It is not farfetched to assume that sensitized persons may have their brain cells tuned into a specific radio frequency and so become susceptible to suggestions coming to them through the ether. Or, to put it more plainly—it is entirely possible that a man might be driven insane by radio waves specially attuned to his brain cells."

"But how about death, Doctor?" Wentworth asked. "Could that be achieved also—almost instantaneous death?"

"Madness is often a destruction of the brain cells," Palmer answered. "If that destruction were complete enough and swift enough there is no reason why almost instantaneous death

should not result. It would be a question of producing radio waves sufficiently strong to shatter the brain cells."

So radio could be turned into a deadly weapon… A weapon even more effective than a knife or a gun… That cast a new significance on the potentialities of a radio engineer—and

Wentworth's thoughts flashed to Melvin Gillespie and his curious behavior.

"You know Melvin Gillespie very well, Doctor?" he switched

That half-second had given

Wentworth a chance to draw his gun!

his questioning. "You have treated him, I believe. May I ask what you think of his mental condition?"

Spencer Palmer hesitated. He was obviously reluctant to betray the confidences of a friend and patient. But Wentworth pressed him, assuring him that the question was for Gillespie's own good and to help his daughter.

"I am worried about Melvin," the psychiatrist finally admitted. "His mental state has not been a healthy one for some time. As you probably know, Russell Gillespie's engagement to Grace Robinson was broken off by the girl's father because he wanted his daughter to marry the wealthy and socially prominent Charles Eaton. You know what happened after that. Melvin never forgave Joab Robinson for it. He blamed his son's death on that broken engagement and hated the Robinsons with an intensity that at times bordered close on dementia."

He protested. "I realize where your thoughts are carrying you, Mr. Wentworth. Such a mania *might* have led Melvin Gillespie to murder the girl and her father—that is possible. But certainly not a whole church full of innocent people! He is not that bad—far from it."

Spencer Palmer might be right in that conclusion, but, nevertheless, when Wentworth left the psychiatrist he determined to have a look at Gillespie's establishment—which might be even better than reaching the old man and questioning him. He took a taxi to Woodside and located the Gillespie home, reconnoitered the big house and found a rear basement window that was partially screened by a clump of bushes.

ONCE HE had reached the cover of those bushes, it was an

easy matter to pry open the window and let himself into a dark cellar room. The place into which he dropped proved to be a bin of some sort. The door was secured by a wooden tongue that dropped into a slot, but the catch snapped when he threw his weight against it.

Beyond that door was a dark corridor that led to the cellar proper; a corridor lined by several similar doors—and then by one that was much stronger than the others and was held shut by two stout metal bolts. Curiously Wentworth drew the bolts and cautiously opened the door on a crack, just sufficient to turn the beam of his pocket flash through it.

The spot of light traveled over bare floor and walls, over a rough bench, and then came to rest on a crude bunk on which a man lay sleeping—a man dressed in rumpled evening clothes. Carefully Wentworth focused the light on the wall just above the sleeper's head—and in the reflected glow he recognized the Vandyked face of Fleming Trask, the deaf organist of St. Stephen's!

Trask, a prisoner here in Melvin Gillespie's home! And still in the clothing he had worn the night of the tragic wedding—which meant that he must have been brought right here when Joan Gillespie and Carl Winkler whisked him off in the girl's coupé....

Trask slept on, and Wentworth drew the door shut, shoved the bolts back into place. There would be time for him later, after the rest of the establishment had been explored.

The remainder of the cellar offered nothing of interest, and Wentworth climbed the stairs to the floor above. Noiselessly he opened the door and stepped into the hallway—but his caution seemed unnecessary. The house appeared to be deserted. Room after room, he worked his way through it, until he reached the rear and stepped into Gillespie's laboratory.

The big room was a maze of electrical equipment of every description. Motors, batteries, generators, and radios of every sort and in every stage of construction. With the perplexed eyes of a layman Wentworth looked them over as he walked from bench to bench—and then stopped in front of a large pen filled with rats. Rats in a radio engineer's laboratory?

He was standing there puzzling over that peculiar circumstance when suddenly he caught a sound outside in the corridor. Footsteps. Someone was coming toward the laboratory!

Quickly he glanced around and discovered a tall, switch studded Bakelite panel behind which he could conceal himself. No sooner had he dived behind it than the door opened and Melvin Gillespie came in.

Straight to a machine that stood on a bench in the center of the room the old man went, to adjust and putter around with it for several minutes. Satisfied at last, he stepped to the rat pen and took down a foot-square cage that hung on the wall above it. This he fastened to the bottom of the pen, opened a door and drove several of the rodents into it. Lifting the rat filled cage, he placed it on another table about twelve feet from the first, then went back to the machine and switched on the current.

Wentworth caught the sound of a low hum that was hardly audible—but his eyes followed the old man's gaze to the rat cage. The instant the power was turned on the captives went berserk. Lashed into frenzy, they fought the strong wire barrier frantically.

Only for a second—then they dropped to the floor of the cage and were dead. Melvin Gillespie groaned, and Wentworth saw that his face was working, his head shaking sadly. Again he returned to the pen and drove a fresh supply of rats into the emptied cage. This time he spent nearly ten minutes regulating the machine before he was ready to turn on the current—and this time only two of the imprisoned rodents leaped madly into the air when the radio beam played on their cage.

Instantly Gillespie's face was transformed. A delighted smile spread over it and a chuckling murmur came from his lips.

"I knew it—I knew it!" Wentworth caught his words. "It could not have gone wrong unless someone meddled with it."

A little to the left he turned the projector—and another rat was caught in the maddening beam. A little to the right— and two more were trapped by it. Now his gratification was complete—but before he could go on with his experiment the telephone suddenly interrupted him.

A frown wiped the pleased smile from his features the instant the bell rang; a frown that Wentworth, watching him intently, could see was fraught with sudden panicky fear.

"Yes," he spoke tonelessly; and Wentworth saw the color drain out of his face as he listened, saw perspiration bead out on his forehead, his eyes flare into stark terror.

At last the old man could stand it no longer.

"No—no—you can't do that!" he gasped. "You can't deliberately murder thousands of people! Please," he begged abjectly,

"I have done everything you demanded. But I never would have furnished the installation if I had thought that you were going to put it to such a terrible use. Thousands of innocent people—you can't deliberately slaughter them! Please don't put this monstrous thing on my soul!"

Wentworth listened with tingling ears, and what he heard sent chills in relays up and down his spine! Gillespie was pleading. His voice was a broken whimper, and tears were trickling down his twitching face—but suddenly he gasped, flinched as if he had been dealt a physical blow.

"Yes… yes… I understand," came hopelessly from his white lips; and now his face was stony and expressionless, almost the face of a corpse. "You know the answer—I will do what I am told. My hands are so deep in murder now that I cannot turn back."

Listlessly he dropped the receiver back onto its hook and slowly turned to the rat cage—but before he could reach it Wentworth was in front of him, barring the way.

"**ALL RIGHT,** Gillespie, don't be alarmed," he said quickly. "I am Wentworth—Richard Wentworth. I am here to help you out of this trouble you are in—to help you fight these devils that have hold of you. Take me into your confidence. Let me know what it is you fear."

For an instant he was certain that incredulous hope flashed in the old man's eyes. Then it was blotted out by unholy terror. The white lips clamped shut as if he would bite back any words that tried to force their way from them.

"I don't know what you are talking about," he said at last; cold dead words that were utterly lacking in conviction. "I don't know what you think you have discovered by breaking into my house and eavesdropping on me, but you are wrong. I was talking about rats, nothing but rats—"

Wentworth was watching him keenly, missing no slightest nuance of expression in that emotion-wrought face—and only that attention saved his own life. The sudden flare of wild alarm in Gillespie's eyes warned him, and he flung himself to one side and to the floor—just as a gun roared from a few feet behind him.

At the last moment Gillespie shook off the paralysis that held him, but then it was too late. He tried to duck to one side, but the bullet caught him in the shoulder, dropped him to his knees—and then another smashed through his chest and toppled him to the floor.

That half-second had given Wentworth a chance to draw his gun. Leaping to his feet, he closed with the short, swarthy thug who had downed Gillespie. Their guns roared simultaneously. Wentworth saw the killer reel backward, saw him start to fall—and then a blinding pain seemed to split his skull into a thousand fragments. This was no bullet pain, he knew even in that moment of agony. Bullets sear like hot irons, but this—

Again that fearful pain enveloped him—a stunning agony that was blotted out by a burst of blinding radiance that seemed to burn right into his eyeballs. A sickening pain that sent him down... down....

It was the biting tang of smoke that brought Wentworth back to his senses—smoke that filled his nostrils and caught at his throat. Smoke that sounded a wild alarm in his brain and forced him to fight down the nausea that overwhelmed him when he lifted his throbbing head. Blood had trickled down into his face from a nasty cut in his scalp—and that was probably the only reason he was still alive. The killers who knocked him out had thought that he was dead and left him there to burn with Melvin Gillespie.

Melvin Gillespie… Wentworth got to his knees and looked around the laboratory. Gillespie lay a few feet from him, a dead man. But he was *not* dead! His eyelids were fluttering weakly, and gasping noises were coming from his lips. He was still alive, and realized his danger.

"Fire!" he gasped. "They set the house—on fire!"

Somehow Wentworth got to his knees and blindly staggered over to the old man. Somehow he grasped Gillespie under the armpits and dragged him out into the hallway, then to the rear of the building, where there seemed to be less smoke. And then he remembered Fleming Trask, helplessly imprisoned down there in the cellar!

He fought his way dazedly through the billowing smoke to the basement—only to find that the cell door was open, the organist gone. Then back upstairs again to where he had left Gillespie. But now the old man was almost dead. He realized that the end was at hand—that it did not matter now about the flames.

"No use!" he gasped. "Go ahead… don't wait… I can't move again."

But Wentworth had gotten a fresh grip on himself. Now his

faculties were functioning clearly again, and he remembered why he had come to that house; remembered what he had heard in the laboratory.

And Gillespie remembered, too. Now the terror was gone from his eyes, and death tore the seal from his lips....

"I AM half mad—I know that," he gasped, "but I am not—a coldblooded murderer. I intended to kill Joab Robinson and his daughter... I admit that. They deserved killing. To do that I perfected a radio vibration beam... a beam that would kill a man by shattering his brain cells... kill him almost instantly. That was to be... my revenge. And the night of her wedding... that was a fitting time... to repay them for sending Russell out to his death. That was why I used *his* song... why I coupled it with the radio beam... so that they would know it was his revenge... before they died."

He shuddered. "I arranged that equipment very carefully... in St. Stephen's. Rigged it up so that only the Robinsons would be caught... in the fatal ray. Just when he was giving his daughter to Eaton—that was when I intended to kill them both. A microphone in the church would let me listen in—tell me just when to turn on the current. But somebody tampered with it—somebody found my equipment and increased the beam terribly... made the death orbit reach out over the whole church.

"Somebody made me a mass-murderer, Wentworth!" In his frenzy he half-raised himself on his hands, and the life-blood cascaded from his lips. "Somebody did that to me—and then held the threat of exposure over my head. I was afraid, Wentworth... afraid of the electric chair... afraid of the disgrace for

Joan. With that threat always over me, what could I do? Nothing. Nothing but what I was told. Nothing but provide the means for all this diabolical killing. I had to obey... and my lips were sealed," his voice was no more than a bare whisper. "But now it doesn't matter...."

"Who is that 'somebody?'" Wentworth pressed, as he cradled the dying man's head in his arms. "Think, Gillespie—don't you know who it is?"

The deep-sunk eyes were glazing, the torn chest barely moving. Death was very close, but the gasping whisper still came.

"Don't know... for sure," Gillespie managed. "Don't know... Only think... Carl... Carl...."

"Carl Winkler, your assistant?" Wentworth bent close.

"Winkler," the old man repeated. "But I don't know. Only know a voice calls me... on the telephone... tells me what to do... what will happen if I don't obey. Same voice you heard calling me... same voice that called earlier today... made me stay here and wait... wait until those murderers could reach here... and kill me...."

The glazed eyes closed and the gray head fell back limply— but he *couldn't* die yet! Wentworth propped him up, shook him, put his lips close to the old man's ear.

"That slaughter of thousands of people you talked about over the phone... where is that going to be, Gillespie?" he pleaded. "Where? When? Try to speak, man! You *must* tell me that—*you must help me stop him!*"

Melvin Gillespie was, to all intents, a dead man—but his

blood-flecked lips quivered ever so slightly, and a bare whisper escaped from them.

"*This afternoon,*" Wentworth caught; and then, "ball game… Yankee Sta—"

A torrent of blood gushed up into the tortured throat and choked the last word before it had been more than half uttered— and with that crimson flood Melvin Gillespie's life passed. But his last desperate effort had been sufficient. Wentworth understood—all too well.

The murderous attack was to take place that very afternoon at the World's Series baseball game in the Yankee Stadium! The World's Series game, where thousands of spectators would be gathered—thousands of unsuspecting victims, ready for a ghastly slaughter!

Wentworth glanced at his watch. It was one o'clock—and the game would begin at one-thirty!

LEAVING GILLESPIE'S body there in the path of the oncoming flames, he raced out of the back door of the building, skirted through the grounds to avoid the crowd that the arriving firemen were bringing with them, and at last managed to locate a drugstore telephone booth. But when he called the Yankee Stadium there was no answer.

The wire was dead—cut, no doubt, so that there would be no possibility of a last-minute warning.

But somehow they must be warned. The police—they would be able to stop this massacre, to disperse the crowd before death reached out and claimed them. But even as that inspiration came to him he realized its utter impracticability. Even if he contacted the police, how could he tell them what to guard against when he did not know what it was himself? How could he hope to convince them that they should disperse the huge crowd gathered to see a World Series baseball game—merely because some unknown person intended to kill them all by means of a song?

CHAPTER 8
FIFTY THOUSAND VICTIMS

WENTWORTH STOPPED in that drugstore only long enough to make a quick purchase. Then a taxicab sped him to the Yankee Stadium. Every block of the way his brain was churning more busily than the wheels beneath him, desperately striving to solve the ghastly puzzle Melvin Gillespie had tossed into his lap. Someone had taken the hellish invention of that poor, hate-warped mind and was exploiting it horribly.

But who was that someone?

Could old Gillespie have been right in his suspicion of Carl Winkler? Winkler was, at that moment, a bed-ridden patient in Dr. Rogers' hospital. He could not possibly have murdered Gillespie and set the house on fire to destroy all evidences of his guilt....

James Leary—could he be the fiend who, somehow, had gotten control of that terrible weapon? Was he now using it with cold-blooded ruthlessness to establish himself indisputably as the racket overlord of the entire city? Had it been Leary using the weapon against his own underlings there in the hotel where Angel McCabe and his companions had died?

If not Winkler or Gillespie—who else could the murderer be?

At last the taxi reached the Stadium, where a few stragglers were still filing through the turnstiles. Wentworth was out of the car in a bound, thankful that he was not too late. Death had not yet struck—but it might be hovering over the densely packed stands at this very moment!

He had no ticket and the box offices were closed, the park sold out to capacity. But a ticket was of no moment now. He *had* to get inside without a moment's delay. The gateman would have to listen to him.

"Get me to your chief immediately," he commanded when he readied the nearest turnstile. "I don't want to see your game. This is a matter of life or death for every man in this park. They may be killed at any moment, unless we can get them out in time."

But the ticket taker regarded him with cynical amusement.

"That's a good line, bud," he grinned, "but it don't get you past me without no ticket. No tickee no inskee—see?"

"I don't want to get into the stands," Wentworth tried again. "I only want to reach your boss. Take me to the office—anywhere where I can reach someone in authority."

Two special Stadium policemen had ranged up behind the husky ticket-taker, and now one of the regular bluecoats stationed on the outside of the ball park was coming over to investigate the disturbance. Wentworth tried again, tried desperately to make his warning convincing—but the knot of uniformed men around the gate grew larger, until they drew him to one side so as not to block the turnstile.

"What's this about the Song of Death?" a regular police

SPENCER PALMER

MELVIN GILLESPIE

FLEMING TRASK

sergeant, in charge of the outside detail, demanded with sudden suspicion. "What do *you* know about that, anyway?"

"I can't tell you that—can't tell you anything definite." Wentworth realized the uselessness of trying to make them understand; already he could see himself headed for the precinct station house and a talk with the captain—while death was closing down on that park to snatch fifty thousand unsuspecting victims! "I simply know that it will strike here this afternoon and wipe out every man in that park unless we warn them. We've got to get in there and spread the alarm before it is too late."

"No, you don't!" The sergeant stepped forward determinedly and grabbed him by the coat

lapel. "You're not running in there and yelling any alarm like that. Want to start a panic? We'd have such a stampede hundreds of people might be trampled to death. Just cool down and take it easy. If you really know something about this Song of Death we'll call out the reserves and throw them around the park—"

It was hopeless! He could not tell them how the menace would strike when he did not know himself—but he did know that throwing a cordon of reserves around the stadium would only add to the number of victims. Now the sergeant was tugging at his coat, leading him toward a police car that had drawn up at the curb.

Once they got him into that

CARL WINKLER

JOAN GILLESPIE

JIM LEARY

car the spectators in the Stadium would be doomed! But they *mustn't* take him away!

"Wait a minute, Sergeant," he resorted to emergency tactics. "I happen to be one of Commissioner Kirkpatrick's deputies. Perhaps if you take a look at this—"

His hand reached inside his coat, down into a vest pocket, and came out with what appeared to be a small card case. The sergeant looked down at it curiously—and staggered back, sneezing and sputtering, when a cloud of blinding dust was hurled up into his face.

Wentworth was past him in a moment, an automatic in his hand as he pounded through the entrance and swept by the thunder-struck ticket taker and guards. For a moment they gaped after him, too surprised to move. Then they came to their senses and took up the pursuit. Wentworth heard their yells behind him; heard them calling to others to head him off. He saw gray uniformed figures closing in on him from the runways that led into the stands, saw them blocking his way, cutting him off—and then he veered to one side and dived into the labyrinth of passageways beneath the stand.

Straight for the players' locker room he headed, to spring past the surprised doorman before he could be stopped. Barely had he found an open locker and wedged himself into it when the special police were swarming into the place, while ransacking it in a thorough search that promised to reveal him sooner or later. Cautiously Wentworth watched them from a narrow crack—and then he saw his opportunity.

Springing out quickly when his end of the room was momentarily deserted, he yanked the door open and let it slam just as he wedged himself back into his hiding place. And the ruse worked.

"There he goes!" the doorman yelled, and the guards stampeded after him to chase the supposedly fleeing fugitive.

WENTWORTH WAS momentarily safe, but now he knew that he had no chance of reaching the playing field—and that was his only hope of attracting the attention of such a vast audience. The runways would all be guarded, and in a few minutes the searchers would come back to give the locker-room a more thorough going over. There, within a few hundred feet of those unsuspecting victims, his lips were hopelessly sealed—until inspiration suddenly flashed into his brain from the very locker in which he stood.

A baseball uniform hanging from the hook beside him—that was the solution! Quickly he stepped out and stripped off his clothing, pulled on the uniform, the stockings, shoes, and cap. On the locker floor was a fielder's glove—and he was completely equipped.

Nobody attempted to stop him as he left the clubhouse by the runway that led out onto the field. The special policemen hardly noticed him. Their attention was absorbed out there on the diamond, watching the play that sent the packed stands into a frenzy of cheering.

A base hit! The centerfielder came running after it, recovered the ball and whipped it back into the infield—and nobody paid any attention to the solitary figure who walked up to the barrier and stood looking out onto the diamond. So far so good—but Wentworth's nerves were on edge. What should he do next?

How should he warn these unsuspecting thousands of their danger? How should he make them believe him—make them understand that he was not a crackpot who was suffering from hallucinations?

Somewhere in those crowded stands death was hovering—but *where?* And how would it strike?

It was a low humming that caught his attention and shouted the answer into his tingling ears. An airplane overhead, sweeping down over the stadium. An airplane that was flying much lower than it should—and coming still lower!

That plane had no business there—none except to broadcast horrible death from the sky!

Instantly, Wentworth galvanized into action. Leaping over the field barrier, he raced out onto the turf and into the diamond. A shout went up from the spectators as they thought a new pitcher was coming in from the bullpen. But the players turned to stare at that unfamiliar figure in amazement.

Wentworth raced past them, straight up to the umpire, who regarded him in bewilderment. Before the official could anticipate his intention, Wentworth had reached the public-address system, had snatched up the microphone and turned to the stands.

"Listen to me carefully—and don't let yourselves be stampeded!" he shouted to the suddenly silenced spectators. "You are in great danger—every one of you! Death is going to rain down upon you from the sky—from that plane overhead—at any moment! The Song of Death that has already slain so many victims—you will hear it at any second! No—no! Don't get into a panic!" His voice rose in stern warning as some of them started up from their seats to bolt for an exit. "Pull your coats over your heads and plug your ears. Then take it easy as you go to the exits. You will be safe if you don't lose your heads!"

A storm of booing arose from the incredulous ones, and a swarm of special policemen started across the park toward Wentworth—but at that instant the first bars of the Song of Death beat down upon them from the amplifier in the low-swooping plane!

Instantly, that great audience rose as a man and started for the exits. Most of them had heard and understood Wentworth's directions. They obeyed as well as they could—but wild panic swept all reason from thousands of others. They swept up the runways in a savage, senseless rush—and soon hundreds of bodies were being trampled underfoot as terrified yells mingled with the resounding doom from overhead.

At the first sound of that fatal melody Wentworth had sealed his ears with a pair of rubber plugs such as swimmers use, which he had secured in the drugstore. Holding his hands against the sides of his head as additional protection, he tried in vain to get the stampeders to follow his example—but now there were few who still looked his way. Nearly every eye was turned toward the jammed runways and the exits.

He was sick at heart as he watched that panic spread; as he watched hundreds, who had come there for wholesome enjoyment, yield their lives beneath the trampling feet of their frantic fellows—and watched others turned into raving madmen before death reached out for them. Most of the spectators would escape the deathtrap because of his warning, it was true—but for the slaughter of those others there was no excuse. Grimly he added their deaths to the long account the murdering fiend someday must pay.

That fiendish killer and his fellows were still at large—and Wentworth knew well enough that they would go from one excess to another. This time he had been able to thwart a whole-sale murder that would have stunned the entire nation. Next time he might not be so fortunate. And the next outrage prob-ably would be even more fearful than this was to have been—unless he succeeded in putting an end to the menace for all time....

THE BALLPARK was almost empty and the murder plane was gaining altitude, its deadly work finished, before he climbed over the railing and picked his way between the corpses that littered the runways. The clubhouse was deserted when he reached it. Quickly he stripped off the player's uniform and got back into his own clothing, to join the head-swathed strag-glers who still were battling madly to fight their way past the corpse-clotted gates.

Past the body of the gateman who had tried to stop him, past the contorted-faced corpse of the sergeant he had tricked, he hurried—and could do no more than cast them a pitying glance. They were beyond human help, beyond aid of the warning they had refused to heed. But there were others who must be saved....

First of all, Wentworth had decided, he would get in touch with Carl Winkler—but when he called the Rogers hospital a startling surprise awaited him.

"Winkler is no longer here, Wentworth," the physician told him. "He broke loose this morning—a short while after he received a telephone call. His nurse noticed that the call excited him, but he lay back in bed and closed his eyes as if he was going to sleep, so she thought nothing of it—until suddenly he leaped upon her and nearly strangled her. Another nurse heard the noise and went to investigate, but he overcame her also. He bound and gagged them both and then knocked out my intern, before he slipped out and disappeared. What time was that? It must have been a little before noon, as far as I have been able to judge."

A little before noon—that would have given him ample opportunity to reach Melvin Gillespie's laboratory in time to have murdered the old man and set the building on fire....

"I telephoned to tell you about it, but you were not at home and neither was Miss van Sloan," Rogers was saying.

Nita not at Sutton Place? As soon as the call was finished, Wentworth dialed his own number and waited with growing apprehension for the connection to be completed—only to receive the message he dreaded.

"Miss van Sloan is not here, sir," Jenkyns' voice came over the wire. "Neither is Jackson. They left several hours ago when Miss Joan Gillespie telephoned and asked for help."

Joan Gillespie—a cat's paw in the hands of Carl Winkler or whoever was behind him! And Nita had been baited into their trap!

All that afternoon Wentworth combed the city for a trace of Carl Winkler, but his quest was hopeless. Utterly hopeless because he did not even know where to begin; had no slightest idea where Winkler might be found. Nor was he any more successful in trying to locate Jim Leary. The politician had vanished from all his old haunts.

Tired and discouraged, Wentworth gave up the search at about eleven o'clock that night and went back to Sutton Place. The quiet street was empty and so still that the sound of his footsteps rang hollowly in his ears as he walked from the corner to the entrance of the apartment building that gave him access, through a dummy apartment, to the stronghold in its rear.

His thoughts were still busily reviewing his unsuccessful quest, as he stepped to the apartment door and took out his keys—when suddenly his keen ears caught a whisper of sound somewhere there in the corridor. He whirled—just in time to leap aside and avoid the rush of a dark figure that leaped at him from a shadowy corner.

Wentworth stared at that black apparition—and his eyes widened with amazement. Eyes that would hardly believe they had just looked at—the Spider!

But there was no time then for astonishment. Instantly the black-caped figure came charging back, to fling himself at Wentworth and flail at his skull with a revolver. That attack was crude, but it was savagely reckless. It swept Wentworth back and he had all he could do to protect his head; to imprison that wildly swinging gun-wrist and twist it in steel-hard fingers until the weapon dropped to the floor.

Even then, the furious attacker came leaping in; to strike out futilely with his fists while panting gasps tore from his lips. But now Wentworth had him in hand. Quickly he pinned back those ineffective fists, gripped the fellow's arms, and twisted them into a knot so that he could do nothing but bend backward and give way to half-hysterical sobbing.

Only then did Wentworth get a good look at his face and see that the Spider he had captured was Carl Winkler!

CHAPTER 9
IN TERROR'S WAKE

DISARMED AND helpless, Winkler had no choice but to enter that apartment; no choice but to step into the clothes closet that opened onto a stairway leading to the tunnel below. With wide eyes he looked about him, as Wentworth led him the length of that underground passageway and into the elevator that carried them up to the third floor of the rear building.

Now his watchful eyes missed nothing; searched every corner as if he expected to find a way of escape at any moment. But it was not his own safety that concerned Carl Winkler.

"Well, where are you hiding her?" he burst forth when Wentworth led him to an easy chair in the living-room and dropped him into it. "Now that you have me, you might as well let me see her—let me know that she is safe. If she isn't, Wentworth—I swear, by God, I'll kill you the first chance I get!"

"You mean Miss Gillespie, of course," Wentworth nodded, "and I can't say that I would blame you—if I had harmed her. But, as it happens, I have not seen Miss Gillespie—although I have been hunting for her, and for *you*, all afternoon. Somewhere we seem to have our wires crossed, Winkler. I have been hunting you to learn what you did with Miss van Sloan."

"Miss van Sloan?" Winkler was wide-eyed. "I—I haven't seen her since she took me to Doctor Rogers. But I saw you, Wentworth." His bitter anger came back with a rush. "I saw you kill Melvin Gillespie and leave his body to burn to a crisp so that nothing could be proved on you!"

It took all of Wentworth's persuasiveness to convince the young radio man that he was wrong; every bit of his tremendous personal magnetism to calm him and win his confidence. Gradually Winkler's hostility subsided and his anger gave way to a new fear for Joan Gillespie.

"I love her, Mr. Wentworth," he declared. "I've loved her for years. I have always tried to watch over her. That was why I became alarmed when her father began to act so queerly. There was something wrong; I had no doubt about it. I spied on him— and what I learned made me *thoroughly* alarmed. I found that he was perverting his great inventive talent—that he was using it to create a machine that would make him a murderer."

He took a breath. "I did my best to combat him, but it was very difficult. Melvin Gillespie was a very suspicious man. When he caught me in the laboratory, when I should not have been there, he almost discharged me. I think it was only because he feared I *might* have learned of his secret that he allowed me to remain. I tried everything to thwart his murderous plans before he could damn himself and Joan. But it wasn't enough. You know that—after St. Stephen's."

Winkler went on. "I learned of that insane deviltry too late. As soon as I knew, from what Joan told me of his reactions to the news bulletin, that he was the guilty man—I knew I must go to the church and remove any evidence that might remain to betray him. I went with Joan, after the bodies had been removed by the police—but we were too late. We reached the corner of the block just in time to hear the explosion that wrecked the building—and to see Fleming Trask come running out of the wreckage."

He frowned. "We thought he was the bomber—thought that somebody had sent him back to blow up the church to cover Mr. Gillespie. So we grabbed him and took him to Woodside. We got him into the house, without the old man knowing about it, and were holding him a prisoner in the cellar, trying to make him reveal the identity of the man behind him—then you came today and turned him loose."

Winkler's eyes met Wentworth's keen stare, and his lids dropped.

"I thought you did, anyway," he qualified. "Your part in this business puzzled me from the first. At the church I thought you were with the police—then I thought maybe you were the one who blew up the church and were going to hold your knowledge over the old man's head. That was why we tried to kidnap you—to try to wring the truth out of you and make you listen to our story."

He shrugged. "But you know how that ended. It was only dumb luck that I wasn't killed. I did plenty of thinking there in the hospital and thought that I had you figured out right—

until this morning. Somebody telephoned me at the hospital and warned me that Joan was in deadly peril—that an attempt would be made on her life out there in Woodside. So I got out of that hospital in a hurry and grabbed a taxi to her home. Everything seemed to get in our way to delay us—and when I got there it was too late. You were just leaving Gillespie's body, and the house was in flames."

Winkler sighed. "Well, that seemed pretty conclusive. I was sure that you had killed the old man and kidnapped Joan—and I didn't know how to fight you. I didn't dare go to the police for fear Joan and I would be involved with that St. Stephen's mess. And then I thought of the Spider. I had read about the way he stamped Angel McCabe and those others, and the papers said he was the one responsible for the Melody Murders. So I hit upon the desperate idea of posing as the Spider myself. I thought that if I could get the upper hand I could force you to tell me what you had done with Joan, and make you take me to her. But now—"

His voice trailed off despondently, but his account was to have

NITA · VAN SLOAN

more result than he supposed. Wentworth had been watching him keenly, studying his every expression, and busily formulating a plan as he listened.

IF WINKLER was telling the truth, as appeared to be the case, the guilt for the Death Song murders, by process of elimination, came home to James Leary. Wentworth's attempts to uncover Leary's trail had failed completely. But there still remained a way to locate the politician. Where Wentworth had failed, where even the Spider would fail, Blinky McQuade might succeed! And this had now become a case for Blinky.

Undoubtedly Jim Leary had taken refuge in the safe hideaways of the underworld—but the underworld held few secrets from Blinky McQuade, few rendezvous where he could not gain admittance. Once more, Wentworth decided to make use of this third personality that had often served him so well. But this time, when he lost himself in the swarming alleys of that human rabbit warren that was New York's lower East Side, he would take Carl Winkler along!

That would require an intermediate personality, for much of Blinky McQuade's effectiveness depended upon the secret of his other life remaining altogether inviolate. To the underworld Blinky was a safe-cracker who had been through the complete curriculum of the college of crime, even to its postgraduate courses. A safecracker who had almost ended his career when a charge of "soup" had gone off prematurely and nearly blinded him, but who had surmounted the handicap of poor eyesight by training his skilled fingers to do the work of the explosives which he would no longer handle.

Blinky was a queer, secretive, furtive creature who came and went about his business with explanations to nobody; a man with no friends but with dozens of acquaintances who would vouch for him and testify to his ability—that was Blinky McQuade. Nobody in the underworld knew anything about his private life—or was so injudicious as to inquire into it. Nobody in that other, "uptown" world ever would have suspected that the frowsy, unkempt individual who shuffled through the crowded, noisome streets was none other than the immaculate, carefully-groomed Richard Wentworth.

And nobody ever must be allowed to suspect that—not even when, as in this case, it was necessary to work with someone else.

110

"Our paths lay together in this," he told Winkler, when his plans were completed. "Your Joan and Nita van Sloan are undoubtedly together—undoubtedly being held prisoners somewhere. The only way to locate them is to go down among the people who are holding them—down into the underworld. We can be more effective there than scores of police. Tomorrow morning we will tackle the job. Now turn in here and go get some sleep."

Winkler was awake early the next morning, eager to start. But when he came out into Wentworth's living room it was to find a stranger sitting in one of the big easy-chairs, reading the morning papers. It was a slick-haired, oily faced, dandified-looking individual who had all the smooth earmarks of a confidence man and the unmistakably ratty look of a dope fiend.

Winkler regarded him doubtfully and nodded uncertainly. But the fellow laughed, and his laugh was that of Richard Wentworth!

"You don't seem to recognize your old pal Salve Hecker," he grinned, "but you had better get used to him. We're going to take an East Side apartment together—as soon as we can find one sufficiently desirable."

Salve Hecker was very particular about that, but at last he found a layout that suited him. Three dingy rooms on the ground floor of a shabby tenement that seemed ready to tumble down—so they seemed to Carl Winkler, but he did not appreciate the advantages of the windows by which one could make a hurried exit into the back yard, or the low fences that could be easily

111

scaled in order to make a quick trip to the next street should a surreptitious exit be necessary.

Carl Winkler did not appreciate those advantages, but the fat, slatternly landlady did. She sized up the too smooth Salve Hecker—and got her month's rent in advance.

Wentworth grinned as she marched out of the room.

"That means we've passed muster," he chuckled, and then proceeded to outline part of his plans to his companion. "For today, at least, you sit tight here," he finished. "Don't try to do anything until I tell you to—or until I send you word."

From the newly rented hideout he set out through the grimy streets into a neighborhood that was even more congested and filthy than the one just left—the neighborhood where Holian Alley terminates its unsavory course through the slums in an intersection with the equally unprepossessing Pallin Place. At the V point of this dreary junction is Number One Holian Alley, a particularly desirable location because of the tiny communal back court that separates it from the last house on Pallin Place— and provides the denizens of both with a convenient rear exit against emergencies.

Into the dirty, paint-stripped doorway of Number One, Salve Hecker turned, to pick his way through the noxious-smelling hallway and up a flight of creaking stairs to the rear room on the second floor—the domain of Blinky McQuade. Once inside that barren, meagerly furnished room, Salve Hecker quickly went into eclipse. Kneeling in the center of the big bed that was its only worth-while stick of furniture, he pressed against certain spots in the huge headboard so that it opened out and afforded him a completely equipped dressing table and makeup kit.

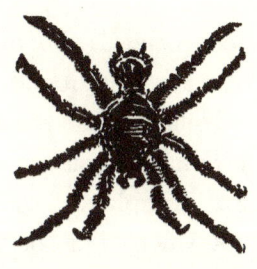

Swiftly his adept fingers wiped away the smug lines that were Salve's, and into their place came a frowsy, unkempt countenance. Sallow, lined cheeks and bristly chin, untidy gray hair, slack lips that hung loosely to reveal discolored teeth, eyes that peered out through thick, metal-hooded glasses—that was Blinky McQuade. When Salve's modish clothes had been traded for a threadbare and none-too-clean suit, and a grimy-collared shirt, the transformation was complete—and Blinky was ready to take his place in the resorts that knew him well.

OUT OF "Holy Alley" he shuffled, scowling and snarling irritably at any who got into his short-sighted way. Into saloons and pool rooms, upstairs into "club rooms" where none but the criminal elite could pass the guardian at the door, into dope joints and hideouts where those who wanted no dealings with the law could be assured of complete immunity, he went. One after the other, doors that were closed to any but the initiate were opened to him—and behind each he was quick to sense a tension and excitement that spelled something of unusual moment in this murky under-current of the great city's life.

Everywhere he found jubilation and grim satisfaction. Money was flowing like water, and everyone seemed to have his share of it. The rackets were flourishing!

"Never seen it to fail, Blinky," Slug Dolan chuckled, when he recognized the unkempt customer who shuffled up to his bar and demanded a shot of whiskey." Whenever times is good you come prowling around."

"Hell—you call these good times?" Blinky spat in disgust.

"What do you want—somebody have to hand you yours on a silver platter?" the burly ex-criminal growled. "I'd like to know when we had better times. This city's just about panicked out of its shoes, that's what. All the boys has to do is go out and collect—with the suckers begging them to take it so that they don't get bumped off. And this ain't gonna be all, either. I'm not saying much, get it—but before long there won't be a business in town that won't come across for protection. Either that or—"

He winked heavily, and Blinky spat again, seemingly too set in his grouch to be cheered even by this promising prospect.

It was the same wherever he went. Here and there, in whispers and in chuckles, he picked up word of racket after racket that was flourishing. Already Slug Dolan's prophecy seemed in a fair way to being fulfilled; already the city's every line of business was coming to heel. Under the threat of inescapable death, merchants and managers of every branch of industry were paying tribute to the collectors without so much as an argument, their "contributions" their only insurance against the dread Song of Death!

Two of the late Heinie Schneider's lieutenants, Moe Goodman and Tarzan Ohlau, were now the underworld kingpins, working hand in glove with Jim Leary, he learned. Goodman and Schroeder, the two who had been convicted with their chief and turned loose with him on suspended sentences, had succeeded Schneider and Angel McCabe, the only one of the gangsters to be acquitted with Leary. In that significant circumstance Wentworth began to see a pattern of cold-blooded scheming and murder.

He could visualize Jim Leary pulling the strings that operated this gigantic campaign of extortion. Jim Leary deliberately staging the murder of Angel McCabe and his companions so that he would have an alibi if the Melody Murders were laid at his door—and, at the same time, shifting control of the gang from the hands of McCabe to those of Goodman and Ohlau, who owed their freedom to the reign of terror of the Song of Death.

Jim Leary, master schemer and ruthless murderer, moving his puppets so that he could dominate them completely....

GRIMLY WENTWORTH resumed the politician's trail, resolved to come to grips with the man no matter what the danger—but even here in the underworld, among the trusted habitués of the most exclusive resorts, Leary's whereabouts were a mystery. Nobody seemed to know where he was or even to have heard of him lately—until Blinky McQuade rubbed elbows with slinking, whining Weeper Miller.

Here was a lead.

The Weeper, as usual, was broke even when everyone else had plenty. As usual, he was cadging drinks; and, as usual, bits of gossip dropped from his lips as he downed his potions—bits which he took a peculiar delight in tossing before his benefactor of the moment.

"Jim Leary—maybe there's a reason why nobody ain't seen nothing of him." He screwed his flabby-muscled face into a sly, knowing mask. "Maybe it's the same reason why he's so anxious to contact the Spider. Not for no trouble—not this time. Maybe Jim Leary needs help. I ain't sayin'—but think that over."

Jim Leary wanted to contact the Spider, to ask his help… Was that some of the Weeper's alcoholic imagining, or was it some more of Leary's cunning scheming; another attempt to reach the nemesis from whom he had thought to rid himself in the Monitor Hotel? It was one or the other, Wentworth decided. Then, when he crossed the path of Whisper Maguire, he knew that the Weeper had not invented the item.

"Seems to me I remember a year or so ago you were supposed to be pretty thick with the Spider," Maguire hazarded shrewdly. "Seems to me I remember he saved your neck once in the Bit House. Yes, that's right, I *know* it now. Don't know how you can reach him, do you, Blinky?" His hoarse voice sank to the barely articulate whisper that gave him his name. "Maybe there might be something worthwhile in it, if you could."

"So that Jim Leary could jump him and fix me up proper for putting him on the spot," Blinky sneered disdainfully and turned back to his glass.

"It ain't like that, Blinky," Maguire pressed earnestly. "Leary wants him—that's right. But it ain't the way you think. Leary wants to cut him in on something—wants to see him *bad.*"

There it was, whispering over the underworld grapevine: Jim Leary was anxious to contact the Spider—peacefully.

It seemed incredible—but Wentworth decided to take a chance.

"I ain't saying that I know the Spider," he grunted. "Ain't saying that I could reach him—but, supposing I did get to somebody that knows him, what's the lay? Where the hell could he find Leary—when nobody else knows where he's hiding?"

Maguire's eyes gleamed and he edged closer.

"I ain't saying that I can find Leary neither," he countered, "but if he knew that the Spider got the word, I know a place where there'd be somebody could take him to Leary."

Again he leaned even closer and mumbled the address of a garage deep in the East Side.

"There might be a gent there about eight tonight that would know," he added—and the conversation was closed.

Eight o'clock—that left almost three hours. Plenty of time for Wentworth to contact Moe Goodman and get another part of his plan under way. From the bar where he left Maguire, Wentworth cut across town to the bail bond office that was Goodman's office and blind. The old man in the front office glanced up and recognized the frowsy caller, grunted something that sounded like a protest at being disturbed then pressed a button at the side of his desk—and the way to Goodman was open.

The thick-set, curry-haired gangster was leaning back in his chair with his feet on the desk, when McQuade shuffled in and blinked at him.

"Hi, Blinky," he grunted from one corner of his mouth as he chewed on the cigar that puffed out his thick lips. "Just the same little ray o' sunshine you always was, ain't you? Sit down and lemme know what's on your mind. I ain't got no safe work for you!"

He chuckled heartily in appreciation of his own witticism, but Blinky McQuade ignored it utterly.

"Don't suppose you ever can use a radio feller, can you, Moe?" he asked almost disinterestedly. "I got a line on a good one—expert. Thought maybe you might have some opening for him."

"Radio feller?" Goodman repeated the words as if the occupation were one he never had heard of. "Don't know what the hell I'd do with him—my radio's okay," he shrugged. "But send him around, if you wanta—won't do no harm to see him maybe."

Goodman's face had betrayed not a flicker of unusual interest. Not a muscle had moved; yet Wentworth was certain that he had caught a gleam of something in the depth of his dark eyes—something that was immediately veiled. Goodman *had* an interest in capable radio men—but whether Carl Winkler would be able to sell himself was another matter....

Winkler peered out through the partly opened doorway in surprise when Blinky McQuade's knock brought him to it.

"You're Winkler, ain't you?" the shabby looking individual asked as he peered through his thick-lensed glasses. "Salve Hecker told me to drop by and give you this address," and he slipped one of Moe Goodman's cards through the opening. "Maybe there's a job for you there. Better go round and see him now—tell him what you can do and that Blinky McQuade sent you, and that's all, see? He don't have to know nothing else."

Winkler seemed to understand that, all right. Glad of a relief from the monotonous waiting that had been his all day; he was already getting ready to keep the appointment when Blinky shuffled away. There was still nearly an hour before eight o'clock and the Spider's rendezvous with Jim Leary—but Wentworth had no intention of arriving at the East Side trucking garage at eight o'clock.

WENTWORTH'S FOOTSTEPS turned toward the East River, but instead of taking him to the rendezvous they led to an old, deserted factory near the shore-front; to a row of sheet-iron garages that stood in the rear of the building. One of those he unlocked and stepped inside, to climb into the ordinary looking, secondhand car it housed. That car would not have attracted a second glance on the street, but its hood covered an engine that could drive it at an amazing speed; and its interior concealed a system of pockets and storage spaces that were stocked with an amazing collection of materials that might serve in an emergency. Blinky McQuade slipped into the driver's seat and switched on a little light above the windshield. That light illuminated his face and enabled him to work in front of the little mirror he propped up on the wheel. Quickly his fingers busied themselves with their task of transformation—and when the car edged out into the black alleyway beside the factory it was the stygian-draped Spider who crouched behind its wheel!

Wentworth's hideaway garage was only a matter of a few blocks from the large trucking company's establishment where there "might be a gent who would know" where Jim Leary could be located. It was seven-thirty, but Wentworth stepped on the gas. A few minutes later he turned into the almost empty side street and drove up to the building. Several trucks stood parked at the curb and the wide doors were open, to reveal half a dozen truck men and mechanics in the interior.

They looked up with a start, when a coupé wheeled in over

the threshold and braked to a sudden stop in their midst. Their jaws dropped and their hands streaked to hip pockets and shoulder holsters—only to stop short in midair. Out of that car had leaped a black, crouching figure that threw himself flat on one of the fenders and regarded them balefully over the muzzles of twin automatics.

"Drop them!" he snapped—and half a dozen weapons clattered to the oil-blackened cement floor.

"Take it easy, Spider," one who seemed to be their leader advised. "We're okay. Nobody would have drawn on you if we'd knowed who you were. We been expecting you—and so's Leary."

From every side came protestations of friendship, but Wentworth kept his guns unsheathed as he followed the leader. Their route led into a rear room and then down a flight of steps to a big basement room, where the apparently solid wall parted weirdly to give access to a little cubbyhole of an office.

Leary sat waiting there. The moment his sliding-door opened, he was on his feet, tense and ready, livid fear gleaming in his eyes as he clutched his revolver. But the moment he caught a glimpse of his ugly visitor, he grinned with relief. Stabbing his weapon back into its shoulder holster, he came forward eagerly, hand outstretched.

"Been trying everywhere to get hold of you." The politician mopped his brow with a handkerchief as he dropped into a swivel chair behind the desk that stood in the center of the room. "I'm in a spot, Spider—a hell of a spot. I know, you think I'm the guy who's pulling these Death Song murders—but I don't know no more about that than you do. Somebody's jobbing me. Killing off all those loan company big shots made it look mighty bad for me."

Now Wentworth saw that the man's hands were trembling, beaded with perspiration. In his restless eyes, in the twitching of his lips, was unmistakable terror.

"Some dirty rat's on my trail, Spider," he gritted. "He's got me on the run, and he knows it. I've got to do what I'm told."

He reached into his inside pocket and pulled out a folded sheet of paper that Wentworth recognized even before it was opened and held out to him. A sheet of music copy paper that was studded with the skeleton-head notes of the Song of Death!

"I got that a couple days ago," Leary snarled, "and the hell of it is I don't dare laugh at it. You can help me. You're the only one who *can* help me—"

Now some of the terror had faded from his eyes.

"That's straight, Spider," he vowed. "I'm not trying to put anything over on you. I need you—bad. Give me a hand with this, and I'll—"

WENTWORTH'S EYES did not leave the politician's face, but his nostrils distended ever so little—and instantly his nerves tingled.

His quick suspicion had been correct—that was gas he smelled!

At that moment Leary caught the odor, too. His eyes widened, threatened to pop from his head. His mouth dropped open, and his whole body seemed to be palsied.

"Gas!" gulped from his trembling lips—and then his voice broke in a scream of terror, just as the lights went out.

Wentworth was not impressed with that demonstration. He remembered Leary's exhibition of terror that day in the Monitor Hotel when Angel McCabe had listened to the Song of Death. Smashing out with his gun, he caught Leary on the side of the head, knocked him sprawling against a far wall—and then whirled toward the concealed entrance.

The Spider did not walk into traps, blindly. When he got ready to accept Leary's invitation he had made preparations for a denouement of just this sort. Out of his pocket he whipped a small, flat grenade that had come from a cache in the hideout coupé—a grenade that went off with a terrific roar when he hurled it at the wall that concealed the sliding door.

Crouched low on the floor, he was ready for the stunning concussion; was on his feet before the tumbling debris had stopped falling, charging out through the gaping hole that a moment before had seemed to be solid wall. Half a dozen killers were waiting out there in the big room to meet him. But the explosion had caught them unawares; had thrown them back on their heels.

Before they were sure what had happened a black phantom came catapulting through the blinding cloud of dust, and the underground room echoed with the thunder of roaring automatics. Two of those killers died before they could get to their feet. Another went down with his skull smashed when he tried to leap at the Spider. But two others reached their objective.

Wentworth smashed down at them with his guns, but one of them had him around the knees. His feet were going out from under him. He was toppling, going down! And then he was on the floor, was being spread-eagled by the two husky bruisers, while a third—Tarzan Ohlau—hovered ready to leap in and finish him.

His guns wrenched from his hands, the Spider seemed helpless. With evil satisfaction the thugs gloated down at him, cursed him vilely as they pressed his shoulders to the floor—and gave him just the purchase he needed. Suddenly his whole body seemed to go into action, to swing upward—but with his feet, instead of his head, on top.

Like twining pythons his legs went into action and fastened around one of the killers—to sweep him from his feet and send him sprawling headlong. In the same instant his body whipped up and over in a back somersault—and he was on top of the other surprised thug; was hammering his face into a bloody pulp.

That was when Ohlau, his great arms stretched wide, came leaping into the fray—only to find himself suddenly whisked from his feet and flung across the room, halfway through the shattered wall. Before he could get to his feet the Spider was upon him, smashing his head back with a blow to the jaw and then clutching at his unprotected throat with steely fingers—fingers that sank deeper and deeper, that squeezed tighter and tighter, as Ohlau strained in vain to break loose.

"Too bad you never took the trouble to learn something about *jiu-jitsu*, Tarzan," Wentworth gritted. "Trouble with you hoods—you know how to use a gun—and that's all. And now—"

At that moment Ohlau's wildly clutching fingers encountered one of the dropped guns, and his eyes flamed with triumph. Perhaps he only knew how to use a gun—but with the cold feel of a weapon in the palm of his hand there were few who could equal him. The automatic whipped around, centered on Wentworth's side, his breast. The tightening finger constricted on the trigger, pressed down—but when the gun roared its mark had unaccountably shifted, and its bullet stabbed into Tarzan Ohlau's own body.

Ohlau's eyes were wide with amazement as he felt the chill of death steal over him. There, above him, loomed the ugly face of the Spider.

"*Jiu-jitsu*, Tarzan," the cracked voice croaked in his ear. "It's better than all your guns!" That voice was bitter. And before the last breath of life gasped from his lungs, Tarzan Ohlau felt something cold press down briefly in the center of his forehead. Although he would never see it, he knew that he bore the crimson stamp of a better man than he, the Spider....

Leaping up from beside the limp body, Wentworth smashed the muzzle of his recovered automatic into the face of the last groggy survivor of that brief battle. Then he sprang through the shattered wall, into Leary's office, his pocket-flash lighting the way. But again the slippery politician had made his getaway. His office chair lay overturned where he had sprawled head over heels—and there was no sign of him in the cubbyhole.

His guns ready for instant action, Wentworth retraced his steps up the stairs to the main floor of the garage. Crouching low, he darted out into the big front room; but now it was deserted. Nobody attempted to stop him as he ran to his car and slipped behind the wheel, as he backed out of the garage and headed the car in the direction of its sheet iron shelter.

124

Once more slippery Jim Leary had escaped—but now he would know that there could be one reward for his treacherous double crossing. Now he would know that between him and the Spider there would be relentless war until one or the other was blasted into his grave!

CHAPTER 10
THE SPIDER HORDE

RELENTLESS WAR—AND how barbarously savage that was to be New York learned the next day, when an all-eclipsing horror burst over the appalled city. At nine o'clock that morning, the entire student body of the Patrick Henry High School, one of the largest in Manhattan, was gathered in the auditorium for the weekly assembly. The music director had announced the first song, was leading the opening verse—when suddenly a strange melody floated out over the volume of young voices; a weird melody that swelled in power until it blotted out all other sound.

The dread Song of Death!

Its irresistible hold fastened upon the doomed students; gripped them so tightly that when the principal, arriving late in the hall, realized what was happening and tried to stop it, he was powerless.

"Stop! Stop!" he shouted wildly as he sprang to the center of the proscenium platform. "Get out—all of you! Get out of this hall!"

But they stared at him dazedly, unable to move a muscle—

until terrible madness contorted their faces and flung them at one another's throats. Helpless, he stood there, his hands clamped over his ears, and watched that sea of fine young boyish faces become transformed—watched nearly two thousand raving maniacs tear and rend one another before merciful death cut short their intolerable agony and dropped them in windrows in every part of the auditorium!

Richard Wentworth sat with Carl Winkler, in their squalid East Side rooms, when the ghastly news of that schoolboy slaughter came over the little radio they had added to the apartment's meager furnishings. On his lap lay the morning papers— papers that shouted the story of the relentless march of the lethal Song of Death.

Eight more prominent, wealthy men had died during the previous day, murdered—cut down inexorably, with the skull-noted score of the murder song in their hands or lying nearby to taunt them and warn them that all hope of escape was useless. Four others had impoverished themselves trying to satisfy the greedy demands of the fiend who had fastened his blood-suckers upon them—and then had committed suicide when they had nothing more to give to protect themselves and their loved ones.

A dozen deaths in a day! But that was only part of the ruthless campaign of terrorism now beating the entire city to its knees.

Those victims were men of wealth—but the thirty-five victims in the station house of the Twelfth Precinct were poor men. Thirty-five patrolmen on reserve duty, they had been trapped in their sleep—slaughtered before they could fight their way to the door. Every man in that building had been wiped out!

Thirty-five policemen ruthlessly murdered as a horrible example to their brothers on the force—and to teach the panic-stricken public that they could expect no help from the police!

And now, swift on the heels of that outrage, came this horrifying high-school tragedy....

As he listened to that appalling news being broadcast, Wentworth could visualize its inevitable effect. The city, already in the grip of mortal terror, would be prostrated, its last vestige of opposition to the demands of the gangster horde swept away in a wave of anguish and all consuming terror. Now New York would pay with its every dollar!

"The police are as good as nothing," Carl Winkler groaned. "But they can't be blamed—nothing can stop this fearful scourge. Melvin Gillespie gave them a weapon that is invincible—a weapon that may beat the whole nation into subjection!"

New York City's police protection had broken down utterly; there was no denying that. But this was not the end, Wentworth swore grimly. The police had failed—now it was up to the Spider!

Now it was up to the Spider to embark on the final phase of the plan he had promulgated when he brought Carl Winkler down there into the stronghold of crime.

For that purpose he worked over his face very carefully, and when he was finished all trace of Salve Hecker's smooth smugness was gone. In its place was the honest face of a good, solid citizen; a face to inspire confidence and respect. When he had donned a conservative, dark gray suit, the transformation was complete. "John Stebbins" was a man of consequence; a man who might be expected to take the lead in civic affairs, in lodge doings or in business organizations. A man anyone would trust—and listen to.

John Stebbins was the sort who could enter a grief-stricken home even though he was unknown to the bereaved family; who could make his sympathy felt, and at the same time reach out and stir the pulses of those whom he wanted to arouse. And before that night he had plenty of opportunity to prove himself....

ONE AFTER the other, he visited hundreds of stricken households and looked at the still faces of young lads who had been cut down in the full promise of their youth. One by one, he talked to the fathers and brothers of those martyred high school boys, sounding them, testing them, evaluating them.

"Your boy died because the men of this city have not had the courage to put an end to these murdering outlaws, because we have not had the courage to fight them with their own weapons," he said softly.

Keenly he watched the saddened faces of his listeners; and when the tear-dimmed eyes flashed with sudden fury, when hard jaws squared and clamped shut grimly—then he spoke further.

"Unless we have learned our bitter lesson and are no longer willing to sit by and watch the slaughter of our innocents," his voice prodded at them; "unless we are willing to band together and undertake the task that has proven too great for the police... If we could do that—then your boy would not have died in vain."

Intently he watched their reactions. And when they wanted to know what they could do, how they could help, and who would lead them, he whispered the name of the Spider and gave them the address of the East Side tenement where Salve Hecker had his apartment.

One by one he enlisted his men, until, at the end of the second day, he had a force of nearly two hundred whom he was certain he could trust—two hundred grim-faced men who had seen their sons and brothers ruthlessly sacrificed so that a great city would tremble and hand over its wealth lest a similar fate strike again and again. One by one, he made appointments for them to meet the Spider in Hecker's apartment—where again he questioned and tested them before committing them to the program.

That program necessitated other preparations, as well—necessitated the purchase of an old, closed up factory near the East River and the leasing of an empty storage warehouse on Broadway, in the fifties. John Stebbins completed those transactions, and then Wentworth was ready to go.

"There is one thing these devils fear—and that is the Spider," he told his recruits. "So we will give them plenty of the Spider. You are going to be Spiders, each one of you Spiders who will harass the crooks at every turn."

Carefully he coached them in the Spider's technique, taught them how to apply the ugly, fear—inspiring makeup, equipped them with the black cape and hat, the straggly wig and bushy brows—made them replicas of the criminal nemesis whom all the underworld knew and feared.

Two hundred Spiders—he turned them loose on Jim Leary's gangsters; used them to strike at the racketeers with telling effect.

One after another, the racketeers' collectors, laden with the day's harvest of extortion, began to disappear. Suddenly, when their rounds were almost completed, they would find themselves face to face with a black caped, snarling visage of the Spider—and then the underworld knew them no more.

So vital were these ravaging attacks on the golden stream that flowed into the gang coffers that soon the collectors traveled only with an escort of several alert bodyguards to watch out for trouble. That system served for twenty-four hours—and then the amazed guards found Spiders swarming all around them! Not one, but three, four and five Spiders, who cut them down unmercifully if they attempted resistance, but disarmed them and forced them into light trucks if they yielded quietly.

Those trucks headed for the newly purchased East River factory, where they ran in under a shed to unload their cargo. On the loading platform more black clad Spiders waited to receive the captives and drag them inside, where they were bound and gagged and then nailed up in packing-boxes and crates—ready for their trip to the storage warehouse.

There, in the very heart of Manhattan, with the throbbing life of Broadway a mere stone's throw away, they were immured in the bleak-walled, windowless structure that was a veritable fortress. That old warehouse was the Spider's prison, manned by hard-eyed Spider keepers who were as grim as their leader.

In less than a week, the satisfied smiles had disappeared from the faces of those who gathered in the underworld dives. Fear had come into the murky depths of their eyes—the fear that makes a man look over his shoulder as if he expected something to pounce out at him from the darkness. The morale of that racketeer organization was cracking, was crumbling badly—and by then, Wentworth knew, the master killer must know that his dynasty of death was toppling.

That could not go on for long. Soon the murdering fiend must be driven out into the open....

FAILURE IS a disheartening thing to face. The realization that every effort has been in vain, that a carefully built organization is going to pieces in front of one's eyes—men have committed suicide when faced with that stark realization. And Police Commissioner Stanley Kirkpatrick faced it squarely, unmistakably. Despite his every effort, the efficient police machine that had been his pride had failed lamentably.

"It's hell, Frank!" he swore fervently, as he paced Mayor Renwick's office. "Men appeal to me for help and I promise them safety—and they die despite every precaution we take. With police all around them, they go mad and drop dead before they can be snatched to safety. Others do not even bother to call us. They disdain police help—would rather impoverish themselves to meet the greedy demands that are made upon them than take a chance with the threat of the Song of Death. And I don't blame them. We can't help them—and I admit it."

The startling tragedy that enveloped the Twelfth Precinct proved to be the proverbial straw that broke the camel's back. Cunningly planned to shatter the morale of the police, it succeeded completely. The force became demoralized, helpless, the threat of inescapable death hanging over every precinct station and haunting the men when they stretched out on their cots and tried to sleep—death that might reach out for them from anywhere and drive them mad before they were fully awake....

From that morning Kirkpatrick could see his fine organization crumbling before his eyes. Men deserted, left their jobs and disappeared from the city. Others tramped their beats like automatons, but might as well have been miles away, for their eyes were closed, their ears shut to anything that might bring the wrath of the racketeers down upon them.

"We might as well throw away the keys to the cell doors!" the commissioner raved. "We can't even hold a man twenty-four hours!"

It was that night that the doors of the Tombs were opened wide and two hundred prisoners walked out without a shot being fired! Helpless, the terrified guards watched them go— and then went with them to escape the wrath of their superiors!

That brazen jail delivery completed the utter rout of the forces of law and order. Crime ran rampant, and the defenseless city turned in its extremity to a weirdly outfitted band of modern vigilantes—the Spiders!

"A lawless band of masqueraders who have taken justice into their own hands," Kirkpatrick dubbed them bitterly—and he writhed as he saw how the desperate citizens turned to them for protection.

"There is one other alternative," Renwick reminded him. "I can call on the governor to put the city under martial law. I am not at all sure that I ought not to do that at once, without wasting any more lives—"

"Without wasting any more lives!" Kirkpatrick snatched the words from his lips. "To bring troops here would mean the slaughter of thousands of helpless men—don't you realize that? Soldiers would be no more effective than my own men—and they would be far more vulnerable. They would die like flies in their armories when the Song of Death reached out for them. This is no job for the militia, Frank. It is a job for the Police Commissioner of the City of New York—and I am going to see it through!"

A gallant boast—but the next morning it was flung back straight into Stanley Kirkpatrick's teeth!

THE NEXT morning, when he stepped into the foyer of his apartment, he spied a white envelope that had been slid under his door. It was addressed to him. Carefully he ran a letter opener under its flap and shook out on his table a folded sheet of paper that shouted its message at a glance.

A sheet of music copy paper that was studded with the death's head notes that had spelled doom for so many victims!

Kirkpatrick had seen all too many of those cryptic warnings—but now that his own lay there before him he felt a chill trickle down his spine. The master of the murderous Song of Death seemed to be clairvoyant—or else he had eyes and ears everywhere. Kirkpatrick's boast was less than twenty-four hours old—and here, grinning up at him in leering skull notes, was his answer: the warning that he was slated for death!

"That warning did not slip under my door of its own accord," he scowled at the local precinct captain, when that official came hurrying in response to his summons. "Someone entered this building and put it there—and I want to know who that someone was! Find him for me, Cameron. Find him and we'll have the Song of Death licked!"

Captain Cameron did his best. He questioned and cross-examined the doorman, the elevator men, the switchboard operator, the superintendent, the cleaners, every tenant who had entered the building after Kirkpatrick came home—but in every case the answer was the same. Nobody had seen a stranger; nobody had the slightest idea how the death warning could have been delivered. The total result was—nothing.

Chewing on his rage, Kirkpatrick made a belated start for his office and the conference of department heads, state trooper officials, and leading citizens that awaited him there. Those state troopers were on hand against his wishes, but the crime wave had spread beyond New York City; had lapped out over Long Island and Westchester. The troopers were there on the governor's orders—precursors of the militia Kirkpatrick feared.

His mind was busy with the approaching conference, busy trying to decide upon the best way of handling these state men. He strode to his office door—and stood stock-still the moment he opened it. Something had happened there in the outer office! His secretary lay slumped grotesquely over her desk—and in the door of his private office sprawled the body of Terry Madden, his personal bodyguard!

Kirkpatrick's face blanched and cold fear clutched at his heart as he sped across the outer office and stepped over Madden's body. Not a sound came from inside his office—where at least fifteen or sixteen people should be waiting, should be talking over the problem that had brought them together! With suddenly icy fingers he grasped the knob and turned it, pushed open the door—to stare into a ghastly *morgue!*

The entire company had been wiped out! Their faces twisted in agony, their bodies contorted, the clothing half-ripped from them, they lay where they had fallen on every side!

The Song of Death had struck—and, but for the delay at his apartment, he realized, he would be lying there with them!

Kirkpatrick fully realized the storm that would arise, the moment the news of that daring massacre, here in the middle of police headquarters, became known. Before the deluge could engulf him, he made swift plans. Establishing himself in another office, he called in four of his most reliable men—men who had risen from the ranks with him.

Joe McGure, Ed Hamilton, Henry Piening and Gus Dorfman—four grizzled police veterans; hard-eyed and tight-jawed, they faced him and marveled that he was still alive. Kirkpatrick met their glances—and knew that they would follow him anywhere!

"These murdering rats have had the brazen insolence to come right here into headquarters. Now we are going after *them!*" he outlined swiftly. "We are going to follow them right into their own filthy sewers and lick them there. I have sent for Lippy Kemler."

The stool-pigeon arrived shortly.

"A nice, easy job—for anyone who's ready to kick off," he made his acid observation, when he heard what was expected of him. "I guess you know what my neck would be worth if it got out that I was tied up with such a stunt. But," he considered thoughtfully, "I ought to be able to pull it. You will have to get decent makeup. Then go down around the Five Corners and find a flat—two would be better for five of you. When you're set you could contact me in Morty Wagner's bar."

Kirkpatrick followed that program. By afternoon he and McGure were established in a pair of furnished rooms, while the other three located in a dismal flat a block farther down the same narrow street. Lippy Kemler jotted down the addresses and promised to go to work.

He was as good as his word. The next afternoon he made an appearance.

"Louis Schwartz is one of the racket collectors," he informed them. "One of the best, he handles the big shots. He's out making his rounds now—and his last stop will be at the Friendly Service Loan Company, on First Avenue and Sixth. He'll get there about six-thirty, quarter to seven. Plenty of dough on him—and he'll have two bodyguards, besides the driver. That's the setup."

IT WAS plenty. At a little after six, Kirkpatrick and his men were in place, hidden in doorways, or mingling with the sidewalk crowd, their eyes on the entrance to the building that housed the Friendly Service Loan. At six thirty-five, a car drew up near the entrance and a jauntily dressed young fellow who had all the earmarks of a high pressure salesman, hopped out of it. He glanced up and down the street briefly, and then stepped into the building. Out after him came two other men. One of them leaned through the car window and chatted with the driver.

The other strolled over to a storefront and became absorbed with the merchandise on display.

Kirkpatrick gave the signal. His men closed in—waited. A dozen or more men came out of the building, by ones and twos—and then Louis Schwartz came striding across the little lobby, a thick Manila envelope under his arm. Kirkpatrick tensed—but before he could lead the way to spring his trap, something happened that was not at all on the program.

Out of a coupé that stood directly in front of the entrance leaped a twisted, stooped figure that he recognized instantly—the Spider!

Gun in hand, the black-clad apparition sprang at Schwartz and seized the Manila envelope; wrenched it from beneath the collector's arm and whirled back to his car. In the same moment the guards came to life. The fellow at the store window fired—but his bullet missed its mark. The one at the car grabbed for his gun, but the Spider swung at him savagely and swept him off his feet. Then, his way clear, he leaped toward the open door of his coupé.

That much Kirkpatrick glimpsed in a split-second—and, even as the swift action developed before his eyes, he sensed that there was something queer about it; something unconvincing. Then he had it! They were *faking* that holdup—which meant that *they were in league with the Spiders!*

Before the black-caped figure could dive into the coupé, Kirkpatrick was out on the sidewalk, blocking its way. The menacing automatic roared, and a bullet fairly brushed Kirkpatrick's cheek—but now his own gun was in his hand, was flaming as his bullets found their mark.

The Spider staggered, stumbled back against the car—and Kirkpatrick was upon him, smashing the revolver barrel down over his head. But now the killers had gone into action without pretense. Their guns were roaring, were clearing the street of terrified spectators. Kirkpatrick saw McGure go down with blood pouring into his face; saw the man who had killed him die with one of Gus Dorfman's bullets in his brain. He saw Piening go down; saw Ed Hamilton's gun drop from his fingers as he clutched at his shoulder.

Now only Dorfman was on his feet, but the driver of the racket car was behind him, was drawing a bead on the back of his head. Kirkpatrick's finger tightened on the trigger, and the treacherous gun dropped from the dead killer's nerveless hand—just as Dorfman made an end of the second bodyguard.

A pall of unnatural silence hung heavy over that hushed street as the firing ceased. Grimly Kirkpatrick looked around him—and his heart contracted as his eyes fell on the slumped body of the Spider. Could this be Wentworth? Quickly he stepped to the prostrate figure, turned it so that the ugly face was exposed—and discovered that the man was not yet quite dead.

Breath was still gasping from his lips—from the lips of Jim Leary, the politician!

And Jim Leary talked.

"I wanted to reach the Spider—to beg him for protection," he gasped. "I *had* to reach him—that was the only chance. I faked this holdup with the boys—let word of their route get out so that it would reach the Spiders. I was gambling on the chance that they would show up here—that I would be able to contact them in this make-up and get them to take me to their chief. But it didn't work. I failed."

And with the realization of his failure mocking at him, Jim Leary died.

As Stanley Kirkpatrick looked down at the dead politician, he realized that his own desperate plan had been no more successful. He and his men had been used as nothing more than cat's paws. Now it was clear that the master killer, whoever he might be, had deliberately had them notified of this rendezvous so that they would come there and kill Leary—and thus eliminate a weak and dangerous link in the criminal organization!

CHAPTER 11
SILENCED CITY

THE NEWS of James Leary's death filled Richard Wentworth with amazement. Leary dead—in a Spider costume? That seemed impossible, and he wondered whether the newspaper account might not be a hoax, a clever trick by which the politician hoped to discourage further search for him.

If Leary was not the guilty man behind the Song of Death, who could the fiend be?

Meanwhile the ghastly terror sank its claws deeper and deeper into the nearly paralyzed city. Radios everywhere were stilled; were disconnected if not actually ripped out for fear the lethal song would come over their wires. The haunting fear of death was in every eye.

Wentworth watched the steadily mounting terror with hard, bitter eyes. All around him a helpless city cowered—and his best efforts were as nothing against the criminal tide. The Spiders worked untiringly. But they were so few against so many; and their activity appeared only to spur the diabolical master murderer to more horrible outrages.

Carl Winkler had been doing his part with the others, but his attempt to insinuate himself into the Goodman organization apparently had been a failure. Moe Goodman had talked to him, had jotted down his address and promised to keep him in mind; but nothing came of it—until a ferret-eyed youth called to say that Goodman wanted to see him.

Winkler answered the summons eagerly, and he did not return....

When there was no word from him by the next morning, Wentworth started to look for him. In the guise of Blinky McQuade, he went to the bail bond office, but Goodman was not there and his man professed to have no idea when he would return. From resort to resort Blinky made the rounds, but Goodman was in none of them, and nowhere did he pick up a trace of Winkler.

All day he persisted in his quest, until seven o'clock found him at the bar of a cellar resort in the rear of what appeared to be a low-type Bowery lodging-house. A pimply-faced youth came in a few minutes after him and ordered a rye... another... and another.

Wentworth eyed him keenly and decided that he must have been up to some devilment that was still very much on his mind. Then the bartender came back.

"I asked Joe," he grunted. "He ain't seen Moe Goodman either. He ain't been in all day."

Instantly the pimply-faced one came to attention. His eyes bored into Blinky's suspiciously.

"What you want Moe Goodman for?" he wanted to know.

"Supposed to see him," Blinky growled. "Hell of a guy!" he spat disgustedly into the sawdust heap beside the bar. "Makes a date and then lets a feller cool his heels half a day waiting for him. Wonder he couldn't tend to business!"

The suspicion faded in the youth's eyes, and Wentworth, watching him, sensed that he wanted to talk. He poured himself a drink and shoved the bottle across the bar.

"Thanks," the young fellow nodded and filled his glass. Then, "You ain't the only one," he mumbled. "There's a lot of guys looking for him—and I come pretty damn near not being one of them! Pretty damn near checked out, I did." He rubbed his nervous fingers over his left ear as if to assure himself that it was still there. "Geez, I can hear that slug whistling past me even now!"

"We was coming in tonight," he confided in a husky whisper. "Stopped to make a last call—and there, I'll be damned if that Spider outfit didn't jump us! One of them stuck a gun in my face, and the damn thing went off before I could hardly move. Burned my cheek with the powder, the dirty rat! But we got him—got three of them and left them lying there on the sidewalk."

Instantly that room became a howling bedlam—a ghastly

shambles where men fought and died!

This was one of Goodman's mob—one of the collectors or bodyguards… Wentworth got him to down two more drinks and loosened his tongue even more before he glanced at his watch and realized that he had to leave. Before he reached the upper door and stepped out onto the Bowery, Wentworth was after him, trailing him carefully.

DOWN A side street the youth led the way to the door of a building that housed a laundry on its first floor. Wentworth's nerves tingled. This place, he was certain, was a gang rendezvous of more than ordinary importance; the youth had intimated as much in his indiscreet talking.

It might even be the headquarters of the Song of Death!

Barely able to restrain his impatience, Wentworth watched. He saw a car draw up a few doors down the street; saw three men get out. One of them carried a satchel—Tony Santaloni, a well-known member of Heinie Schneider's mob!

This place *was* a headquarters—a gathering-place for the collectors! And where the money was, the head of the outfit was very likely to be!

This was the chance to corner the murdering devil!

But how? It would be too risky to go in there alone; too likely to give the fellow a chance to escape. Wentworth must be certain that there was no chance for a slipup. He must have help—from the Spiders.

From a drugstore booth he telephoned the factory and asked for every available man. Ten were there to answer his call. They would come at once. While he waited for them, Wentworth stepped into a sedan that was parked near the laundry. It was the only shelter he could find that would enable him to watch the street. It would have to suffice while he put on his make-up and donned the Spider's well known habiliments.

Alertly he crouched there until two cars passed him and drew up at the curb—two cars from which ten black-caped figures hurried the moment he stepped out and gave the signal. The side door of the laundry, he had already ascertained, was open. Stepping inside quickly, he held it back while that weird looking company filed through.

Then, cautiously and noiselessly, he led the way to the rear, guided by the low murmur of voices in the distance. Eleven stygian specters were gliding along a dimly lit passageway, through the quiet workrooms from which the workers had gone for the day. Now they went down a flight of steps to a basement corridor. The voices were louder, coming from a room just ahead. A transom was over the door.

Boosted by two of his men, Wentworth pressed close to the dirty pane. Through it he could distinguish a score of men gathered around two others who sat at a long table—two tellers receiving the day's collections and checking them off in ledgers. And there, in a seat that was raised above the others, sat a black robed and black masked individual who watched them like a hawk—greedy eyes observing that stack of currency grow higher and higher.

Wentworth pressed his ear to the window, tried to distinguish what they were saying. Then suddenly that room became electrified! A bell was ringing—and instantly the tellers were up out of their seats, sweeping the money into two suitcases. The thugs were whirling toward the door, hands streaking for their guns.

Someone had given the alarm! Too late, Wentworth heard the sound of footsteps on the floor above, on the stairs.

"Inside!" he snapped. "Shoot out the lights—and then let them have it!"

With a rush they swarmed through the doorway, undismayed by the leaden hail that greeted them. Eleven almost identical Spiders—with twenty-two guns roaring.

Instantly that room became a howling bedlam, a ghastly shambles where men fought and died in a welter of blistering gun-flame and smoke. Carefully Wentworth sighted at the over-head lights. Two of them. They disappeared simultaneously—and then the table lamp went down and was ground to pieces on the floor. Blackness enveloped the room—blackness pocked by what seemed to be a myriad of stabbing orange flames.

"Be sure of your men before you shoot!" he yelled above the din. "Grab them first—be sure they aren't wearing capes!"

Then he was through the press, diving toward that raised chair where the masked man had been sitting. He reached it—just as the chair went over backward. For a moment his fingers closed on the fellow's black robe, but it tore, left him clutching a piece of cheap muslin. His quarry was gone, escaping in the darkness.

Wentworth had to have a light; had to chance the beam of his pocket-flash. But when he snapped it on it was too late. The spot of light stabbed at the empty chair, past it at the farther wall—which was just settling back to the floor, closing the gap beneath it. The masked leader was gone—and so were all of his fellows who were still able to follow him. In a split second the wild hubbub subsided and the room was filled with a silence that now rang in Wentworth's ears.

"Upstairs!" he commanded quickly. "Get out before we are trapped down here!"

The Spiders left in a rush. But before he followed them he ran from one sprawled corpse to another. His cigarette—lighter stabbed down—and each time the crimson mark of the Spider leaped out on the forehead of a dead thug. With the two money loaded suitcases in his hands, he pounded up the stairs after his men and flung himself through the open door of the car that waited.

With a roar, it sprang from the curb and whisked him off into the Bowery traffic.

Four Spiders had died in that savage struggle—but they had not given their lives in vain. Even though the murder chieftain had escaped, this raid upon his collection headquarters would be a sorry blow to his prestige and to his hold over his men. Now they would know that he was not invincible; now they would know that the Spider was on his trail—would know that he was doomed!

Surely, now he would be driven out into the open….

Wentworth's prognostication was to be realized even more swiftly than he expected. At midnight that night a strident radio voice boomed out over the silenced city, issuing a terrible ultimatum to any who might be courageous enough to be listening in. And the next morning the newspapers repeated that dire warning in bold, black type that leaped out startlingly from the white pages.

"To the Spider and the City of New York!" it shouted. "Notice is hereby given that you have until three o'clock this afternoon to release every one of my men who is being held prisoner—both in the city jails and in the private jail of the Spider. If this order is not obeyed to the letter by the hour specified, the death penalty will be inflicted upon the entire city! Obey by three o'clock—unless you want to listen to… the Song of Death!"

JOAN GILLESPIE'S frantic plea was still ringing in Nita van Sloan's ears as she turned away from the telephone in Wentworth's Sutton Place home. Joan had promised to call if she needed help, and now she had—but Nita was not at all sure of the motives that had prompted the girl. She had undoubtedly been greatly agitated, perhaps terrified—yet something about her plea had not rung altogether true.

"Miss van Sloan!" she had gasped over the wire. "I need you terribly! I have been trying all morning to reach you—but this is the first chance I've had to get to a phone. I have been kidnapped—no, not just kidnapped; I was forced to come here. If I hadn't, they threatened to expose my father and send him to the electric chair."

"Who forced you?"

"Oh, I *don't know!*" the girl had sobbed brokenly. "Nothing but a voice on the telephone—but that was enough. I *couldn't* hold out against such threats—I had to come here. And now I'm afraid, terrified! This is a madhouse I am in, or worse! They are beasts, these men. They watch me constantly! I can see terrible things in their eyes!"

"But what can I do for you?" Nita had puzzled. "Give me the address and I will bring the police."

"No! Not the police! Not that!" the girl's response was instantaneous. "If you could come for me—if I could see your car outside in the street—I think I could get away. I have that much freedom; I could run out to you. *Please* do that for me, Miss van Sloan! *Please* come and get me before they kill me!"

Nita and Jackson drove over the Queensborough Bridge to the edge of Sunnyside and located the address the girl had given. It was a large, old-fashioned house that stood close to the street which had been cut through what, formerly, had been its grounds. An empty house, from the lack of any sign of life around it.

Twice Jackson passed it slowly in the car, while they regarded it dubiously. On the third trip, Nita suddenly grasped his arm. The stillness of that almost open country had been broken by a shrill, terrified scream—Joan Gillespie's' scream!

"Careful!" Jackson warned as he jammed his foot on the brake. "That may be nothing but a trick to—"

But his words died on his lips as he stared at the house. Now there was life behind one of those downstairs windows. Suddenly the shade was snatched away, torn loose from its roller, and the Gillespie girl was revealed. Half naked, she struggled in the arms of a burly thug; struggled so frantically that she tore loose and hurled herself at the pane.

It shattered, and she tried to leap through the frame. But a cruel whip licked out after her, wrapped around her neck and shoulders. A peal of utter agony tore from her lips and she was dragged backward—but not before Nita and Jackson were out of the car and running to the low porch, up the four steps and onto the sagging floor boards.

That floor sagged even more than it should! Nita knew that the moment she stepped on it. But now it was too late to turn back; her momentum carried her forward. It carried her almost up to the broken window before the floor gave way beneath her. Not with the snap and crackle of rotten wood, but as if she had stepped on the end of a seesaw.

The whole floor upended—and she and Jackson were swept off their feet, were shot down into a dark cellar!

Before they could scramble to their feet, heavy forms pounced on them out of the darkness, pinned them down helplessly and lashed their wrists and ankles firmly. Then they were picked up and carried upstairs to a cubbyhole of a room that was little larger than a closet; were dumped onto the floor and left in darkness when the door closed upon them.

"Tricked!" Jackson muttered grimly. "The Major left you in my care—and I lead you into a trap that a kid should have seen through. I—"

Abruptly he stopped and sniffed suspiciously. But Nita also had caught the odor that was stealing into his nostrils.

"Gas!" she whispered, as chill terror raised the hairs at the back of her neck. "This is a gas chamber, Jackson. They are filling—"

And then her senses swam dizzily, and she knew no more....

150

THE SONG OF DEATH

WHEN SHE came back to consciousness the darkness was gone. Strong light stabbed at her blinking eyes and made her roll her head to avoid the direct beams. The smell of gas was gone, too; now she sniffed the medicinal odor that is peculiar to hospitals and asylums. She opened her eyes wide in sudden fright—but the room in which she found herself looked more like an electrical laboratory or a radio workshop.

Gradually the coma-like daze lifted, and she realized that she was sitting in a chair. Her arms were strapped to it so that she could not rise, indeed could hardly move. A short distance from her, Jackson sat similarly confined. Her eyes met his and read the bitter self-condemnation that blazed in them. However, before she could speak a door at one side of the room opened and a black specter stalked in; a man who was clad from head to foot in a black hood and gown.

"So you have awakened?" The hooded head nodded at her approvingly and a deep voice came from behind the mask that hid his face. "We have been waiting for you. Waiting to begin some experiments in which you are to have a part. These are scientific experiments, Miss van Sloan—experiments on the brain. I am sure that you will be interested."

As he spoke he stepped to a machine that resembled a large, many-tubed radio. Carefully he adjusted it and turned it so that several antenna-like rods were pointing straight at her and Jackson. Then he stepped to a tall bakelite panel and grasped a switch, pulled it down with a click.

The moment that switch clicked shut, the room was filled with a peculiar buzzing that quickly increased in volume and

151

rose in tone until it stabbed into her ears with a terrible intensity. That fearful sound was like a knife stabbing into her flesh, like a dentist's drill held mercilessly against an exposed nerve. The agony of it threatened to split her head, flowed down over her whole body in frightful waves that bathed her skin with perspiration.

Nita strained at the straps until her body was taut—but there was no relief. The unendurable agony grew worse and worse—until she knew that she could stand no more. Her senses reeled, a hazy mist came down over her eyes—and then, suddenly, the pain stopped. The awful noise was gone and, as she sagged forward in the chair, that deep voice was speaking again as if it never had stopped.

"I hardly think that you will want to take part in these experiments. It will not be necessary if you are reasonable, and can induce Richard Wentworth to come here and intercede for you. The demonstration I just gave you was merely to give you an idea of what the treatment is like—so that you will be better able to appreciate what our friend Jackson will endure."

What followed was a horrible nightmare. Jackson fought to maintain his self-control as long as he could. But his tortured body writhed helplessly as the devilish rays from that projector stabbed into his brain. Soon his clothing was soaked with perspiration and his eyes had the maniacal gleam of a madman's. Still no sound came from his lips—not until the masked tormentor spoke.

"I believe you understand me, Miss van Sloan," the heavy voice rumbled. "You can put an end to this experiment whenever you wish. All that I ask you to do is cooperate with me in inducing Mr. Wentworth to come here—"

Then Jackson spoke.

"No! No!" he gasped. "No matter what he does to me—don't listen to him! Don't betray the Major into his dirty hands! No matter—"

Again the switch snapped on, and the words were bitten back into his mouth by his tight-clenched jaws. Helplessly Nita sat there and watched him suffer. Helplessly she watched the madness creeping over him—while every twinge of his agony seemed to run through her own body....

IT WAS like that all the days that followed—until it seemed that she had lost complete track of time. Hours at a time she was forced to sit and watch Jackson's ordeal. Slowly, she knew, he was being driven insane.

But that frightful ordeal could not go on forever. Sooner or later, Jackson's mind must snap—and unless she could find some way to save him. Constantly that thought was uppermost in her mind; continually she watched for a chance to escape. And at last her opportunity came—the white-clad attendant who brought her supper was careless.

As he unlocked the door of her cell-like room, he merely glanced at the cot on which she usually sat. There was a huddle of blankets stretched out on it, the edge of her dress hanging out from beneath them, a glimpse of her hair on the pillow—that was sufficient to satisfy him. He turned to put his tray on the bare table—and instantly she leaped from behind the door where she had been tensely crouching. She was on his back, pounding down on his skull with the heel of her shoe.

That shoe was not heavy; it was a mere slipper. But the heel was sharp. The attendant reeled, staggered; blood poured down into his face. Savagely, he whirled and tried to yell for help, but her hand clamped over his mouth—and then the tattoo of blows had its effect. His knees crumpled and he went down. Instantly she was on top of him, gagging him, tying him up securely with strips of cloth she had ripped from her sheet.

Warily, she stepped out into the corridor and traversed its full length to a stairway. Her cell was in the basement. There was no way of escape until she reached the floor above—and then she discovered that every door was guarded, doubly-guarded. To attempt to get past those guards without a weapon of some sort was hopeless—but where could she find anything that would serve her purpose?

The torture laboratory! It was her only hope. There she might lay her hands on a heavy tool that could be used as a club; perhaps she might even find a knife.

Carefully, she picked her way to the room where she so often had been dragged for hours of torment. It should be empty now at the supper hour. But her pulses pounded as she grasped the knob and turned it slowly, noiselessly. The door opened without a sound—and she tensed. There *was* someone in the laboratory!

That someone—was Carl Winkler!

Incredulously she stared at him. No, there was no mistake; that was Joan Gillespie's fiancé. He was busily at work, absorbed with another intricate mechanical contraption that had been set up in place of the usual torture apparatus—another machine that looked like a very complicated radio set.

And now there was a new prisoner strapped to the chair where poor Jackson had suffered such agonies. Nita stared—and again her eyes widened in surprise. That man was Fleming Trask, the deaf organist of St. Stephen's—only now he no longer seemed to be deaf!

Winkler had adjusted the delicate mechanism to his satisfaction; had switched on the current.

Fleming Trask was going mad—raving mad! There, before her eyes, his brain snapped and now he became a hopeless maniac!

That sight was so awful that a gasp of horror she could not repress burst from Nita's lips. Carl Winkler heard her. He whirled. His eyes widened with surprise, with fear. He paled—and then he leaped at her. Too late Nita turned and tried to run. Winkler was upon her, was grabbing her.

But at that moment there was a rush of footsteps in the corridor, and Joan Gillespie sprang through the doorway and threw herself upon him.

"No, Carl—please!" she gasped. "They have made a murderer of my father, but they won't make a murderer of you, too! I won't let them, Carl! I won't!"

Frantically, she tried to drag him out of the laboratory, tried to lead him down the corridor toward the door. Winkler seemed dazed, uncertain whether to go with her or to resist—and, before he made up his mind to flee, the decision was out of his hands. White uniformed attendants came running from every direction. They overwhelmed Winkler and the girls, held them helpless while they were securely tied up. And then a taunting voice, from somewhere down the shadowy corridor, pronounced their doom.

"You are no longer needed here, Winkler. You have served your purpose," it boomed derisively. "For this insubordination all three of you will share the same pleasant fate—and will pray for the Song of Death to put an end to all of your suffering!"

CHAPTER 12
DAY OF DOOM

BY NOON of the day on which the murder master's ulti-matum was delivered to New York the city was in wild panic. Fearful terror gripped the populace and increased with every passing moment. One o'clock... two... two-thirty—they watched the clock with fascinated eyes, like the condemned.

And at two-thirty the self-appointed master of their destinies spoke. His booming voice blared out from every radio that was still in commission, every radio that was being dialed apprehensively for possible news. At the same time a plane winged low over the city, scattering a snowstorm of handbills. The message on the air and on those bills was the same—Radio City broadcasting station was in the hands of the master of Death!

"Two-thirty!" the warning voice reminded. "Remember—you have until three o'clock. Then, unless my orders have been obeyed, the Song of Death will go out onto the ether waves from this station. It will penetrate every building in the city—and you will listen to it whether you want to or not! All the ear stoppers and protective devices with which you have equipped yourselves will be of no use. When the Song of Death goes onto the air you will hear it despite everything!"

Two thirty-five—that left less than half an hour; too little time for Wentworth to rally an appreciable number of the Spiders. This was a crisis he must face alone. Now there was barely sufficient time for him to rush to his East Side hideout garage and fling himself into the commonplace looking coupé. But the moment he got behind the wheel he had occasion to bless the specially built motor beneath its hood.

The streets were free of traffic, and there was only an occasional wildly fleeing car to be avoided. Grimly he stepped on the gas and watched the speedometer needle climb from seventy to eighty, and then up to ninety. Block after block flashed past—and yet Radio City seemed an interminable distance away.

At last he reached it and stopped his car at the corner of Fifth Avenue. From there he could see that the police were laying siege to the great broadcasting building. As he came nearer, he saw that armored cars and machine guns were ranged around it. Barricades had been thrown up on the opposite sidewalks, and police sharpshooters were keeping up a steady fire from the windows and ledges of the buildings that surrounded it.

But the thugs who had taken over the building were well entrenched. Their tommy guns, back in the lobby, commanded every entrance, and a rain of grenades and bombs from the windows kept the police at their distance. To dislodge those defenders would take many hours, perhaps even days—and now three o'clock was only ten minutes off!

In ten minutes, if that terrifying threat was no bluff, doom would sound from that building, would spread out over the entire city—doom that no man, woman or child could escape!

But, somehow, that must be stopped!

Wentworth's feverish brain wrestled frantically with the problem. There was no hope of storming the building's doors; no chance of reaching one of the windows on a higher floor. The place was a fortress that would defy any frontal assault; a fortress from top to bottom.

Bottom—that was the answer! The cellar was the building's vulnerable spot, and the one the gangsters were most likely to have overlooked!

The moment that inspiration flashed into his mind, Wentworth went into swift action. Racing back to Fifth Avenue, he ran into one of the smaller Radio City buildings and hurried down to the cellar, then to the sub-cellar. Here he located the metal door that led to the steam company's main. He paused and took precious minutes to go to work on his face and to don the black raiment of the Spider.

Ready at last, he grasped the metal door and opened it—to find the dimly lit tunnel jammed with terrified people. Women screamed shrilly at sight of his ugly face; tried desperately to fight their way back through the press. Men cursed and moved, uncertainly, to block his way—but the Spider's automatics halted them, his snarling face cowed them.

"Stay back, you fools!" he shouted. "The Spider is no foe of yours! I am here to help you—if you are willing to help yourselves before the Song of Death reaches down here and dooms

158

you! I want men to follow me—as many as dare fight for their lives!"

Out of his pockets and from his belt he emptied a regular arsenal of automatics—twenty of them that he had taken from where they were cached in the coupé. The sight of the weapons, the sound of them clinking on the tunnel floor, gave heart to the terrified fugitives. One man stepped forward and picked up a gun—and after him came a stream of volunteers.

They made way for him and then closed in behind him as he led a course through that maze of conduits. An almost trackless maze beneath the city's streets—it would be so easy to lose the way into those tunnels; and that would mean sure death before the mistake could be rectified....

WENTWORTH LED the way carefully, despite his almost irresistible desire to race with blind speed. Carefully he followed the little indicator signs—and at last he stepped out into the sub cellar of the broadcasting building. It was deserted. So was the basement above. But the moment he led his little band to the first floor he saw that their immunity was ended. That floor was thronged with thugs. But their attention was now concentrated around the entrances and the windows of the sidewalk level stores.

"We must take them by surprise," he snapped his orders quickly. "That is our only hope. Sweep through them and clear a path to the north side elevator. That's the only way we can reach the studios in time."

With a leap he catapulted through the doorway, his guns blasting death before him, his eerie howl striking terror into the hearts of the astounded thugs. After him charged the grim faced volunteers. Twenty automatics echoed his own and added to the din of the chattering tommy guns. Twenty guns that spat death as they swept toward the north side of the building and the direct elevator to the broadcasting floors.

The first of the surprised thugs went down before they knew what had happened, and their death spread instant panic among those who had seen them die. Dozens took to their heels, running wildly for any shelter.

"The Spider! The Spider!" rang out above the uproar—and the panic spread like wildfire.

But that rout was only temporary. There were far too many in that legion of the underworld to be stampeded by a mere handful of attackers. All too quickly they rallied—and Wentworth caught the sound he had dreaded. A tommy gun had been diverted from the outside and was sweeping the corridor. Men went down like tenpins before it. His little force was being decimated… but before that scything lead could mow him down he reached the elevator.

Two minutes to go!

And he did not even know from which studio, which floor, the fatal rendition was to be made….

As if in answer to his dismaying question, a red light at that moment flashed on the indicator at his side. Someone wanted to go down from the first of the broadcasting floors—and that someone would know where the murderous deviltry was being hatched!

Wentworth gripped his automatic and brought the car to

160

a stop at the designated floor. The door slid open—and Moe Goodman started to step inside! In mid stride he realized his error and went for his gun.

Lead whistled by Wentworth's cheek, carried his hat away, lanced through his cape. He did not want to kill Goodman before he had a chance to make the fellow speak—but the precious seconds were flying away. No time now to beat him into surrender. Wentworth fired. Goodman staggered back, clutching at his chest; fired again—and then the gangster dropped to the floor, dying but still conscious.

"You win, Spider—but a lot of good it will do you!" he sneered. "You're licked—and so is this whole damn city. You may be pretty smart—but you're not as smart as the professor. He's two thinks ahead of you and everybody else—all the time. You got me—but you're gonna follow me to hell so fast that you'll be surprised!

"Maybe you've got stoppers in your ears so that you can't hear me?" His face twisted into an unholy grin. "Lot of good that'll do you. You're gonna hear the Song of Death anyway. Why? Because that broadcast is going out on high-power radio waves that will penetrate to your brain without going through your ears! The whole damn city is finished, Spider! Those poor fools running around with stoppers in their ears will be killed without even hearing the death song."

His eyes closed.

LEAPING TO his feet, Wentworth raced down the long corridor, from studio to studio. Which one contained the infernal death broadcasting apparatus? He had no way of knowing—

and there was not the slightest clue to help him! Ears straining for the first notes of that fatal melody, he ran his eyes over the signs on the studio doors—and suddenly a name leaped out at him. A name that was listed on the day's program of broadcasts from that studio.

The instant he read that name his brain began to click at top speed. The "professor" that Goodman had mentioned... A super-thinker... This Machiavellian death trap that yawned for a whole city... One by one, a dozen or more suspicions that had been latent in Wentworth's mind suddenly took concrete form—a dozen suspicions that interlaced to weave a pattern.

Feverishly he yanked at that studio door—but it was locked! Desperately he hurled himself at it from across the corridor; twice, before it smashed open and pitched him halfway down the banked steps of the empty listener's balcony—just as the opening bars of the dreaded Song of Death floated from the amplifier!

Down there in the studio he could see the diabolical machine that was to be the inanimate murderer of a whole city! And, attached to it, the mechanism that was broadcasting a recording of the Song of Death synchronized with the murderous radio rays that would reach a climax on its final shrieking notes!

The wild music was already ringing in his head, but Wentworth fought desperately to ward off its hypnotic effect. With his automatic he battered against the heavy plate glass of the booth front, smashed it to pieces, and leaped down into the studio. The fall jolted him and served to clear his head. He was on his feet again in a moment, was lunging for that murder machine—to hammer and batter his gun barrels down upon it with a fury that made him forget it was not human, only an unfeeling contraption of metal and glass that had sprung to life from a diseased brain.

Wentworth pounded and battered it—but that deadly machine fought back. Its terrible ray fingers stabbed through his skull, reached deep into his brain. His head was whirling, filled with an intolerable pain that seemed to be numbing him. Like an automaton he beat against the hellish thing—but his arms were becoming so heavy that he could hardly lift them. The fiendish contraption was licking him, was beating him down... but at last the dread melody stopped.

But that was only half the task!

Again and again he told himself that, as his suddenly exhausted body craved rest, craved sleep. Only half the task was finished! That reminder hammered through his brain as he rushed from the studio and hurried back to where he had left Moe Goodman.

"Where is the professor, Moe?" he shouted over and over again. "I want the professor—you understand? I want to find the professor. Where is he, Moe?"

"Go to hell—that's where you'll find him!" Moe Goodman jeered with his last breath. "Laughing at the poor fools in the flames!"

CHAPTER 13
HELL'S NOCTURNE

SPENCER PALMER—HE was the professor! He was the fast-thinker, the psychiatrist who was too smart for everyone else! That was what Moe Goodman had meant. It was Palmer's name that Wentworth had glimpsed outside the studio in which the death machine was operating; the studio in which Palmer gave a weekly talk on applied psychology. Bit by bit the murder pattern began to take form. The friend and confidant of the Gillespies, Spencer Palmer had been in a position to work on the old man, to take advantage of his hate against the Robinsons. After Wentworth had called upon him and given evidence of his suspicion of Melvin Gillespie, it was Palmer who had telephoned a warning to Carl Winkler; Palmer who had arranged to have Gillespie murdered and the building destroyed before its secrets could be discovered....

And undoubtedly it was Palmer who had gotten hold of Joan Gillespie and prevailed on her to lead Nita and Jackson into some sort of trap!

Wentworth was certain of his ground now; what a few minutes before had been no more than suspicions now took on the convincing guise of facts. Spencer Palmer was his man—but Palmer's home and office were blocks away, across town. Already, he must know that his plans had misfired. The cessation of that deadly broadcast would have given him warning; given him an opportunity to flee....

But was Palmer the fleeing type? The cold trickle that rippled

164

down Wentworth's spine was his subconscious answer to that question. For a coldblooded monster such as Palmer had proved himself, flight would be the last resort. There were other ways in which he could clear himself of any possible suspicion—ways of eliminating any who might accuse him.

Perhaps already he had put an end to Nita and Joan Gillespie! Was that what Moe Goodman had meant by his cryptic sneer?

That staggering possibility sent Wentworth racing for the elevator that had brought him to the broadcasting floor. Again he sprang to its controls, but this time he directed the car to plummet straight down to the basement. There was nobody to stop him when he opened the door and came out with guns ready. Uninterrupted he ran down to the sub cellar and into the steam main.

"All right—you are safe now!" he shouted to the hundreds of trembling, hysterical women and children who still cowered there. "The danger is past. You can go up on the street."

Then he was through them, retracing his steps of less than a quarter hour before. Fifth Avenue was still empty, the dead street of a ghost town, when he came out onto it and ran to his car. It would come to life again shortly, but whether or not it was to stay alive would depend on what awaited him in the house on East Thirty-Eighth Street. Toward this he drove the coupé at top speed.

That house was Spencer Palmer's office and also his home, a three-story building that stood next to an ornate six-story structure now closed up. The former quarters of the Cornell Club, Wentworth had noticed the name chiseled over the boarded up door—but now he gave the place not even a glance. The moment he turned into Thirty-Eighth Street he had eyes only for the Palmer house.

Like all the surrounding streets, the block was silent and deserted, and the house gave no evidence of occupancy. There was no answer when he rang the bell; no answer when he pounded on the door.

With trembling fingers he jabbed his skeleton key into the door and manipulated the lock. Inside, the building seemed even quieter, more grave-like, than the silent street; so quiet that the almost noiseless closing of the door sounded thunderous behind him. Quickly he scouted through the first-floor rooms. Those in the front were Palmer's reception room and office, behind them his study and living rooms. But he was in none of them, neither he nor any of his assistants or servants.

They were gone, all gone....

Suddenly he tensed. His quick ears had caught a sound that was like a muffled thumping—a sound that came from some-where downstairs, in the basement.

Gun in hand, Wentworth started down the steps, and again he caught that muffled thumping. More clearly this time... it was the sound of someone pounding on a wall or a door.

Like the hallway above, the basement corridor was deserted, but once he reached the lower level he had no difficulty locating the source of the pounding. It was coming from a room at the very rear of the corridor—a restless thumping and pounding against a heavy door that was held fast with several stout bolts.

With the automatic held ready, he pulled the bolts back and

stepped aside. In a moment the door was yanked open, and out of the black room behind it staggered a disheveled, unshaven man who glared around him with blinking, half blinded eyes. A man who stared at the black garbed Spider without the slightest sign of recognition.

But that man was Jackson!

Horrified by that appalling discovery, Wentworth felt the goose-pimples come out on his arms as he gazed at his faithful friend. Jackson—in that terrible condition!

"What happened, Jackson?" He took the dazed man's arm gently and led him over to one of the hall lights. "What have they been doing to you? Where is Nita? Where is Palmer?"

Question after question—but Jackson only stared vacuously. And when he did try to speak, an incoherent stream of gibberish dribbled from his loose lips. The man was helpless; in a mental stupor. Worse than that—he was practically a madman!

Jackson was helpless—and yet it was he who saved Wentworth's life. One moment he stood there staring into space and mouthing nothings; the next, his eyes blazed with mingled rage and terror and he backed away fearfully—backed away from two husky, white clad hospital attendants who had appeared apparently from nowhere.

Wentworth caught that sudden gleam of terror just in time. He flung himself to one side as they leaped upon him—fast enough to elude one of them, but the other reached him and swung at him viciously with a length of heavy rubber hose. Had that blow landed squarely it would have knocked him senseless. Even when he caught it glancingly, he thought that his left shoulder was broken. But the agony of it swung him around like a top and added impetus to the down-sweeping gun barrel that landed on the fellow's skull and smashed its way through the bone.

With a savage curse, the other bruiser closed in to avenge his partner—but now Wentworth was ready and anxious to meet him. That gleam of terror in Jackson's eyes had told its own story.

Whimpering and begging for mercy, the attendant gave ground steadily. But now Wentworth saw that there was method in his retreat. He was heading for the open door of a room nearer to the front of the building. Wentworth followed close—and just as the blood spattered bruiser was about to dive through it, he brought up his fist in a smashing uppercut that dropped his man like a poled steer.

Over the fallen body, Wentworth stepped into the basement room—and saw at once why the fellow had been so anxious to reach it. The farther wall, on the Cornell Club side of the building, was built of stone, apparently solid and in place for many years... but a whole section of it had come loose from the rest and swung into the room like a door. That was how the attendants had appeared so magically.

Beyond that curious doorway was the basement of the untenanted club, and beyond that—what?

Wentworth intended to lose no time finding out—but what was he to do with Jackson? The man was utterly helpless.

Once more he tried to talk to the chauffeur, tried to plead with him; but it was useless. There was only one thing to do— and he did it quickly, painlessly. Putting all his skill into a swift, short uppercut, he clipped Jackson on the point of the jaw, and caught him as he fell, knocked out cleanly.

With that heavy body over his shoulder, he trudged upstairs and out to the coupé. Slumped on the seat, with the door of the car locked, Jackson would be safe even if he revived.

THAT HAD taken precious minutes. Quickly Wentworth dashed back into the house and breathed a sigh of relief when he found things as he had left them. Stepping through the opening in the wall, he picked his way across the adjoining cellar and then up to the first floor of what had been the fashionable Cornell Club. Now the building was bare and dismantled. Dust was thick over everything, and the place seemed to have been long-deserted. Curiously, Wentworth prowled through the empty rooms until he came upon tracks in the dust—tracks that led to the wide stairway.

Noiselessly he followed them, rounded the second floor landing—and then fairly froze as the eerie stillness was suddenly rent by terrified screams from somewhere overhead!

The frightful pandemonium there was almost deafening; seemed to come from a doorway at the side of the gymnasium. Wentworth padded up to it and grasped the knob; eased the door inward gently until he could see into the room beyond— and then stood transfixed with stark horror!

That room had once been a swimming-pool, but now it had become a fiends' playground—a madman's nightmare!

Instead of water that pool was now filled with blazing oil! The dancing flames leaped upward hungrily and cast an eerie, flickering light on a curious arrangement that was raised on a dais at a safe distance from the pool's edge—an arrangement that looked like the console of an organ. But no sane craftsman had built that devil's organ! Where the keys and stops should have been, levers had been substituted—levers that connected with heavy chains strung over a metal beam near the ceiling. And fastened to the ends of those chains were the bodies of half a dozen girls and one man—Carl Winkler!

Wentworth's blood seemed turned to ice as he stared at those agonized faces. He stared at Joan Gillespie—and that of his own Nita! There she dangled with the rest, helpless above that pool of leaping, dancing flames that seemed to be reaching out like greedy live things for the soft bodies that hung suspended temptingly above them.

A devil's organ—and the fiend who bent over the hellish keyboard might have been Satan himself. Wentworth stared at that tall, spare figure in rumpled, disreputable-looking evening clothes. Even before the lowered head raised and turned so that the flames played redly upon his closely trimmed Vandyke, Wentworth recognized Fleming Trask!

The weird melody of the Song of Death drooled from his laughing lips as he manipulated those demoniacal levers like an artist who feels every slightest tone of his music—and with each working of a lever one of those terrified, shrilly screaming victims was raised or lowered above the leaping flames. With consummate cruelty that incredible fiend tortured them, lowering them until the flames licked out and snatched at their squirming bodies, until the fearful heat threatened to snatch away their breath—then hoisting them high just as the limit of endurance had been reached.

Suddenly it flashed into Wentworth's mind that this was what Moe Goodman had meant! This was the hell where he had said the professor would be found! The professor was Fleming Trask....

But there was no time then for debating the "professor's" identity; Nita was being roasted alive!

The chain which held her started to ripple over the bar, started to lower her into the fiery pit, as Wentworth poised, his every muscle ready to spring and hurl himself at that inhuman beast. But he caught himself at the last moment. To leap at the monster now would mean to cause Nita to plummet straight into the raging flames!

By a superhuman effort he held himself in check and watched her flinch from the blistering tongues; watched in an agony of apprehension until Fleming pulled the lever that raised her once more to the ceiling—and then he burst into that inferno in a charge that carried him halfway to the organist. Halfway... but before he could reach the madman, four more of those white clad devils closed in to stop him.

WENTWORTH CLUTCHED two guns, but he became utterly atavistic in that moment. Gone was his cool self-control, his unerring marksmanship. In his raging fury those automatics were no longer firearms; they were nothing more than chunks of metal, no more than rocks such as his ancestors had used to beat out the brains of their enemies.

With a scream that might have come from a charging lynx,

171

the Spider rushed to meet them. The loaded butts of the whips they carried crashed down on his head and shoulders, but his berserk rage rendered him immune to pain. As if those blows were no more than the falling of leaves, he brushed through them and came to grips with the men who would keep him from Nita.

One of them went down with a gaping hole in the center of his forehead! A hole had been battered there by a descending gun muzzle. Another fell back in panic as those bludgeoning weapons hit him. But the Spider was after him in a flash, hammering at his face until his features were nothing but a bloody smear.

Now, two more men were closing in on him from the rear. But just as they reached him he threw himself to the floor and backward; tripped one of them in midflight and plunged him into the blazing pool. Three men had died in less than a minute—and before the fourth could take to his heels, the Spider had him.

Not until then did the red rage ebb from his brain. Sanity returned with a rush—and his eyes turned to the madman who sat at his unholy console as if nothing had happened.

Fleming Trask lived in a world of his own—in a hell that raged within his twisted brain. He neither saw nor heard what went on around him—until Wentworth reached him and yanked him from his seat. Then he resisted with a fierce strength that was almost superhuman… but the Spider had fought with madmen before. Standing off to avoid the maniac's frenzied rush, he beat his fists into Trask's face; hammered him with scientific expertness. The organist's knees wobbled, the mad laugh left his suddenly stricken features—and then he was lifted off his feet, was sent crashing back against the pseudo organ, a limp heap that sprawled over the depraved keyboard.

Wentworth lifted the inert body and dropped it to the floor as he sprang to those devilish controls. Quickly he hoisted the screaming victims clear of the blaze; and then, like a human spider, he sped up the narrow metal ladder that led to the cross-beam, picked his way across it to the first of the suffering victims and hauled her up to safety before he freed her from the chain clamped around her waist.

One after the other, he freed them and helped guide their trembling feet to the ladder and safety. Before he was finished, the heat up on top of that metal beam was terrific. Twice he caught himself as he reeled and almost pitched down into the flames—and then he saw that not only the pool but the whole room was on fire. The madman's bonfire had escaped from the tile and concrete pit and was lapping greedily at the walls, climbing swiftly toward the ceiling.

Was Fleming Trask the fiend who dominated this madman's layout? Was he the master of the Song of Death? Had he murdered Palmer? But those white clad huskies—they were undoubtedly attendants in the private sanitarium Palmer ran in conjunction with his psychoanalysis practice. And yet they were there, helping Trask....

"Get those girls downstairs, Carl," he ordered as soon as he had released Winkler. "This heat will overcome them at any moment. Get them downstairs and stay there with them until I come."

Winkler obeyed with alacrity. One after the other, he helped the trembling captives down the ladder and led them out through the gymnasium; all but Nita van Sloan. She shook her head and insisted upon staying until the last; until Wentworth came down, his task completed—and then she could no longer go!

THE MOMENT his feet left the last rungs of the ladder, Wentworth was grabbed. Out from behind the organ had sprung two more of the white uniformed attendants. In an instant they had disarmed him—and then their master appeared behind them. It was the same black-gowned and masked figure Wentworth had glimpsed in the East Side laundry; the same inhuman devil who had gloated daily over Jackson's agony and Nita's mental suffering.

"So you *are* Palmer," Wentworth flung at him contemptuously. "I thought Trask wasn't capable of degeneracy as complete as this. Take off the mask, Palmer—your rotten soul has been exposed so completely that your face no longer matters."

"Anything to oblige," Spencer Palmer laughed, and he lifted the hooded mask from his head. "I believe it is customary to grant the last request of those who are about to die, is it not? So you knew who I was, did you? Then, perhaps, it will not surprise you, Mr. Spider, to learn that I know you are Richard Wentworth. I had my suspicions for some time—but when you freed Miss van Sloan from her somewhat precarious position you gave yourself away. You were a little too concerned for her safety; a little too careful about the way you lifted her and helped her over the beam."

With a mocking grin he nodded to his men. That was the death signal, Wentworth knew—but he had been tensely waiting, watching for just that moment.

Apparently docile and defeated, he stood there helpless in their hands—one moment. In the next, he had galvanized into whirlwind action. Suddenly his arms whipped up over his head and broke the attendants' grip—and in the same swift motion he had gripped them both around the waist, had lifted them from their feet. Straight toward the pool of flames he staggered—a doomed victim taking his executioners to the grave with him.

They read his mad intention and yelled in wild terror. Frantically they struggled to break loose—and on the very brink of the blazing pit they succeeded. His grip relaxed and they slipped out of his arms. But for one that was literally a case of leaping from the frying pan into the fire. Over into the pool he toppled before he could recover his balance on its edge—and then Wentworth was locked in a death grapple with the other.

Back and forth they wrestled, teetering precariously on the very brink of destruction, the hot flames licking out at their legs. Back and forth... but Wentworth's grip was shifting; his hands were working their way into a new hold that gave him leverage.

At last they were in place. Swiftly his knee drove up into his opponent's groin, his arms shot out—and the hungry flames closed over another screaming victim.

Spencer Palmer had not tried to take a part in that grim struggle; had not even waited to see its outcome. The instant the first of his men plunged into the flames he had taken to his heels. Nita ran after him.

"This way, Dick!" she called from the door of the gymnasium the moment Wentworth was free. "The roof! He is escaping!"

Wentworth was past her in a flash, sprinting out into the hallway, where a flight of steps led to a roof kiosk. Up those steps and out onto the roof—just in time to see Palmer, at the edge, about to lower himself on a rope that he had had in readiness for his flight. Down that rope three stories, and he would be on his own roof—and the way to freedom would be open before him....

His feet were already over the edge when Wentworth reached him and grabbed him by the shoulders. Palmer fought frantically; tried to bite, to scratch at Wentworth's eyes—but the grip on his shoulders was relentless. Back over the edge of the roof he was pulled, back onto his feet—and then Wentworth's fist smashed his face and sent him staggering.

"The electric chair will be too easy for a fiend like you," he gritted. "You should have a taste of your own foul medicine—but civilized people can't resort to flame torture."

Palmer was staring as if he saw a ghost—staring over Wentworth's shoulder. Wentworth whirled—and the apparition he beheld might, indeed, have been a specter from the great beyond!

Fleming Trask had returned to consciousness in the midst of the huge bonfire the entire swimming pool room had now become. Blackened and blistered, his hair singed from his head, his clothing hanging to him only in smoldering patches, he had crawled out of the inferno. Somehow he had managed to drag himself up there to the roof; had dragged himself to a little covered box that stood behind the kiosk. On hands and knees above it, he had lifted the cover, was reaching inside.

"Stop him! Stop him!" Spencer Palmer shrieked in hysterical panic, the moment he could command his voice. "He is going to dynamite the building! He will kill us all!"

"Yes—you are right," Trask muttered. And, when his blistered face turned, Wentworth saw that his eyes were nearly sane—the eyes of a dying man who was clinging to life grimly until he had accomplished one all-important task. "You are going to die, Palmer. This time the double-crosser is going to die in his own trap—with the one he has betrayed!"

Deliberately he pulled the switch in that box before Wentworth could make a move toward him—and then, with an amazing resurgence of strength, he was on his feet; was across the roof and locked in a death grapple with the fear-petrified Palmer.

"Nita!" Wentworth gasped; his arm around her as he was hurrying her to where the rope dangled over the edge of the roof. "Around my neck! Hold tight!"

She understood. Her arms encircled him, clung to him as her head rested on his shoulder, and hand under hand he started downward as swiftly as he dared. One floor—another... At any moment he expected to be blown into eternity, buried beneath the tumbling wall of the doomed building—but they had almost reached Palmer's roof before it happened.

The wall beside them trembled—and Wentworth dropped the remaining distance, just as a terrific roar filled his ears and the entire Cornell Club building disintegrated. Stunned by the fall, he forced himself to his feet, picked up Nita and dragged her to safety before the billowing wall came crashing down onto the roof.

THEY WERE still alive, and now they and the imperiled city were freed from the ghastly threat of the Song of Death… but at a price that might be on Wentworth's conscience forever. His anxious eyes flashed to Jackson's unconscious face as he slipped in behind the wheel and then he headed the coupé to the north. His duty to the city was fulfilled; now he was bound far from the metropolis, to a place where Jackson would find peace and the best of medical care.

As the car sped through the city, Nita pillowed Jackson's head on her shoulder and tried to bring him back to his senses.

"He has been through hell," she said softly, "a hell where the presiding devils fortunately had a falling-out.

"Palmer and Trask," she amplified. "They were originally partners. They planned this terrible crime campaign together. It was Trask who wrote the music of the Song of Death—and Palmer who forged the suicide note that was supposed to have been left by Russell Gillespie when he took off on his suicide flight. That wasn't suicide at all—it was coldblooded murder. His plane was blown to pieces when a bomb that was planted in it exploded—and the man who planted that bomb was Spencer Palmer."

"You're guessing at that, of course," Wentworth said softly, while his mind coped with the enormity of the thing she was outlining.

"No, I am not guessing, Dick," she denied quickly. "I wish that I were—it is a terrible thing to realize that human beings can be so utterly depraved. But while I was a captive in that house I learned a great deal from Joan Gillespie—and from Palmer, himself, when he came to boast and let me see what a clever person he was."

She went on. "Palmer knew the Gillespies, of course. He knew of Russell's broken engagement and saw how it was affecting his father. He knew of Melvin Gillespie's mechanical genius—and he deliberately planted in the old man's mind the idea of devising a safe and dramatic way of avenging his son by murdering the Robinsons. The night of the Robinson-Eaton wedding, coming at the end of the racket trial, was doubly-ideal to introduce their murder weapon to the world. It paved the way for the ultimate blame to be thrown on Melvin Gillespie—and at the same time it was an excellent opportunity for the plotters to horn in on the racketeers and take over their whole organization through a campaign of terrorism."

She frowned. "To be sure that there was no discovery that might incriminate them or throw suspicion on Melvin Gillespie prematurely, Trask slipped back to the church that night and blew it up. After that, Palmer had easy sailing. Schneider's gang and Jim Leary were framed and were pushed into a corner so quickly that they were forced to do his bidding. There was little danger from them, but Palmer was keen enough to realize that you might prove to be his undoing, Dick."

"That was not why we were attacked on our way to the wedding," Wentworth objected. "Nor was it the reason for that attempt on our lives in your apartment the same night."

"No," Nita agreed. "Those attacks were made on Leary's orders—to settle with you for your part in the trial. But they fell in beautifully with Palmer's scheming. After that, it was he who instigated the war on you—and made you think that it was Leary and Schneider."

She nodded. "They were fiendishly clever—I say 'they,' although I should really say 'he,' for Fleming Trask played a minor role in the plotting from the start. It was that fact that turned Palmer against him. Easy money was too much for Palmer. He wanted more and more of it and hated the idea of Trask having an equal share when he was doing so little of the work. He plotted to get rid of Trask and have the whole thing for himself. Trask suspected something of that when he was being held prisoner by the Gillespies and Carl Winkler. When he was 'rescued' from the burning Gillespie home and brought back to New York, he accused Palmer—and the result was that he was handed over to Carl Winkler to be made into the mad thing you saw this afternoon."

"Winkler did that to him?" Wentworth turned unbelievingly. "Winkler drove him mad?"

"I know something of what poor Carl went through before he did as he was told," Nita said softly, compassionately. "He faced the choice of using Trask as a subject for experimentation in producing the high-power ray projector that threatened the city—or of watching Joan Gillespie suffer at Palmer's hands. She would have suffered even worse than poor Jackson—would have been driven completely insane and killed slowly, horribly."

Her face was grim. "I know—it was a terrible decision that Carl had to make; but, when he made it, he already knew that Trask was one of the plotters responsible for that awful massacre in St. Stephen's. I think I could have turned the ray machine on him myself—and felt like a public executioner while I was doing it."

For long minutes she was silent, lost in retrospect, as the car sped from Manhattan to the Bronx and headed for Westchester.

"The end, of course," she said finally, "was to have been Trask's death when the Cornell Club was blown up under him—after he had roasted us to charred crisps. And why did Palmer make him do that? I suppose we shall never know—unless we delve far more deeply into psychiatry than I have. Palmer was a sadist, of course. He gloated over our suffering—but I think there was more to it than that. I think he hated Trask for some reason—and because he hated him, he deliberately debauched him. I think he gloated over Trask's excesses, over the despicable thing he had made of the man, as much as over our agony—"

"Perhaps the Almighty deliberately twists brains that become as rotten as Palmer's," Wentworth nodded understanding. "It was only that that tripped him up. Otherwise," his eyes flashed to Nita's violet ones and looked far into their warm depths, "otherwise we would all be back there beneath the ruins of the Cornell Club now, and Spencer Palmer would be free to enjoy the tremendous fortune he extorted from his victims, without the slightest suspicion pointing his way."

THE COUPÉ was still heading north the next noon when Wentworth stopped at a quiet roadside dining room for a bite of lunch. At least, the place was quiet when they stepped inside, but as soon as they were seated the proprietor, anxious to please, turned on the radio.

Nita's eyes turned to Wentworth, and they were filled with anguish.

"Terrible!" she shuddered. "After what we have been through, I feel that I never want to hear another broadcast. Just the sound of a radio is enough—"

But then she stopped and listened, her eyes wide. It was the voice of Mayor Renwick, of New York City.

"—and so we have the Spiders to thank for redeeming our city from anarchy and destruction," he was saying. "I realize that, to accomplish their purpose, they were forced to take steps which ordinarily could not be countenanced; were forced to commit acts that, under ordinary circumstances, would be criminal. For that reason, it gives me great pleasure to announce that I have before me a proclamation from the governor of this state, in which he completely absolves them from all penalties."

He wound up. "To you Spiders, I want to say this. You have demonstrated that you are men of such caliber that now, the emergency past, you will fade back into the populace from which you sprang—but always you will be a potent force for law and order in our city!"

Wentworth could not restrain the thrill that crept through him as he listened to those words of endorsement and appreciation. But when he turned and looked into Jackson's vacuous eyes, the cost of such loyal service came home to him—a cost that would not be repaid until that faithful friend and ally was completely restored to normal health....